From the Street
TO THE STARS

PRAISE FOR ANDY NEBULA:
INTERSTELLAR ROCK STAR (BOOK ONE)

Nominated for the
Manitoba Young Readers Choice Award

Named to the Our Choice list
Canadian Children's Book Centre

"This book is like Star Wars *plus drug dealers plus rock stars all joined into one book. If you like to read about that stuff then you will love this book…This is a cool book so check it out!*

— *A YOUNG READER*

"The action in Andy Nebula *moves along at a cracking pace and the characters are well-drawn…* Andy Nebula *is fast and furious enough to keep even reluctant readers turning the pages, and young teen fans of fantasy and science fiction will not be disappointed."*

— *JOHN WILSON,* QUILL & QUIRE

"… gritty and clever…Willett tells a fast-moving tale that has plenty of colour. He wastes few words and presents some good characterizations… All in all, a worthy addition to a young reader's shelf of SF books."

— *A. L. SIROIS,* SF SITE

"It's the combination of the familiar with the speculative that lifts Andy Nebula above the crowd…From page one we know we are in another time and place thanks to Willett's deft and never-faltering use of a convincing invented slang…. There's a whole lot of story packed into the pages of this trade paperback…Get one copy for yourself, and another for a young person."

— *DONNA FARLEY*, NCF GUIDE TO CANADIAN
SCIENCE FICTION & FANDOM

"Willett writes in a humorous and flamboyant style not unlike an old-style detective novel…The novel is fast and exciting with lots of action. It also involves broader themes like differentiating between the authentic and the contrived, values and measuring success, drug addiction and tolerance between species…The writing is trim and humorous but far from vacuous. This book is fun to read. Kids will like it, too."

— *JOCELYN CATON*, THE REGINA SUN

**Andy Nebula:
Interstellar Rock Star
Book One**

From the Street
TO THE STARS

EDWARD WILLETT

SHADOWPAW
PRESS

FROM THE STREET TO THE STARS
Andy Nebula: Interstellar Rock Star
Book One

Published by
Shadowpaw Press
Regina, Saskatchewan, Canada
www.shadowpawpress.com

Second edition
Revised by the author
First edition published 1999 by Roussan Publishers

Print ISBN: 978-1-9993827-2-8
Ebook ISBN: 978-1-9993827-3-5

Cover design by Edward Willett
Photo by dwphotos via Shutterstock

AN UNEXPECTED ROOMMATE

COLD WIND LASHED MY FACE. Cold rain dribbled down my back. My fingers throbbed like I'd slammed them in a door, my toes squished in my waterlogged boots, my throat felt as rough as rusty iron, and my nose was both stuffed up *and* dripping, but I kept playing my beat-up stringsynth and singing the best I could. My open case barely held enough soggy cash for a mug of red-bean stew, much less a bed in Fat Sloan's flophouse, and I didn't fancy a night on the streets in this weather.

But the few people who splashed by me on their way into the tube station had eyes only for the dry warmth promised by its flickering blue holosign, not for a skinny, ragged streetkid.

That did it. I broke off in the middle of a soulful, wailing note—it was threatening to turn into a cough, anyway—and flicked off the stringsynth. If I'd sunk to feeling sorry for myself, it was time to lift. Feeling sorry for yourself is just another way of saying you think somebody else ought to be taking care of you. First thing I'd learned after escaping the orphanage seven long years ago was that *I* was the only person I could trust to take care of me.

I fished the thin, dripping handful of feds out of my case, counted them, and shook my head. *Sometimes I can't even trust myself.* Unless I could talk Sloan into a discount, it looked like I'd have to settle for a mug of stew and a night of shivering.

Lightning flashed, thunder quick-marched across the sky, the rain beat down even harder, and I decided to give Sloan the chance to be generous. None of the nearby hidey-holes I knew would be any good at all in this kind of weather—they were mostly under bridges or in burned-out basements, and I knew from experience that if they weren't flooded yet they soon would be. Besides, on a night like this the free spaces would be crawling with rats, both the kind that squeak and the kind that run around on two legs. I could wake up stripped naked and robbed blind—I knew that from experience, too.

Or, I might not wake up at all.

I put my instrument into its soggy case (my ancient, all-metal stringsynth was impervious to rain), slung it over my shoulder onto my back, and started down the street—but I stopped at the first corner and looked back, feeling a strange itch between my shoulder blades.

Under the tube-entrance holosign stood a man in a long black weathercoat, the expensive kind that repels raindrops a full metre in every direction. I ducked out of sight. *Can't be a 'forcer, not with that coat,* I thought, but that wasn't a comfort. The Fistfight City peaceforcers generally treated me all right. Sure, they'd chase me away from a place if they got a complaint, but they didn't say anything when I went back a couple of weeks later. But lots of other people took an interest in kids on their own. I had my music, but a lot of kids had nothing but themselves—and they still had to eat.

Some were on the next street over. They stood in purple-lit doorways, watching for the occasional slow-moving wheeler or talking to shadowy figures uncomfortably like the man in the weathercoat. As I splashed past one of the doorways I heard a man cursing, and the sound of a hand meeting flesh, then muffled sobs that broke off as a door slammed.

Nobody on the street took any notice. *They wouldn't pay any more attention if that guy in the weathercoat grabbed me,* I thought, and broke into a run, ducking into the next alley. Several twists and turns later I arrived at Fat Sloan's, out of breath and shivering. I pushed through the heavy front door into the sour-smelling warmth of the lobby. A man lay unconscious on the shiny, lime-green couch—but only one. *Slow night,* I thought.

Fat Sloan deserved his nickname. A mountainous bubble of bloated flesh, he must have moved off the stool behind the counter sometime, but I'd never seen it and found it hard to imagine. He smiled at me, yellowing teeth showing briefly between pendulous lips. "Young Kit! What a surprise."

I raised an eyebrow at him. "You know I berth here when it's hydrating, gladeye."

Sloan spread his hands and shrugged, which made his neck disappear in rolls of fat. "Busy night, Kit. You want a room, you'll have to share it."

I held up my money. "I've got feds for a single." I didn't even have feds for a double, but he didn't have to know that yet. Maybe I could get him to knock down the price.

"Maybe, but I haven't got a single to give you."

"No flashman roomie for me, Sloan!"

"Kit!" Sloan, attempting to look shocked, put one hand in the general vicinity of his heart. "Would I do that to you? This...fellow...is a perfectly respectable freespacer. He's just between ships at the moment. And I know he'll be happy to meet you."

I didn't like the sound of that. I remembered the street with the purple-lit doorways. "No street-trade either, Sloan."

"Would I even suggest such a thing? This is a legitimate establishment."

Sure it was. "Then what's his interest?"

"He told me he likes music, wants to meet a musician. Didn't know you'd be in tonight when he said that, but here you are. A match made in heaven."

Huh. I still didn't like it—but thunder rattled the door, and rain—or was that hail?—rattled on the window, and the truth was, I'd always wanted to talk to a spacer. If I were ever going to escape this interstellar slimepit, I needed a space-friend. *And if he really is interested in music...*

I didn't let any of that show on my face. If Sloan knew I was actually intrigued, I'd never talk his price down. "Still comes down to economics, Sloan. Fewer feds for a double."

He shrugged. "So sleep in the street."

I put a little wheedle in my tone. "Come on, Sloan, flexibilize for your old gladeye."

He squinted at me for a moment, then grunted. "All right. For you, ten percent off."

"Forty."

"Kit, synchronize with reality. It's raining. I'm a businessman—supply and demand. High demand right now, low supply. Fifteen percent."

"Thirty."

He shook his head. "No deal."

"Nominal with me. I'll REM in the street—and spread the data you're defunct." I turned toward the door.

Sloan laughed, a remarkably unpleasant sound. "All right, Kit. Tell you what—twenty-five percent off. Just for you."

"Orbital, gladeye." I turned back to the counter and paid him, then tossed a couple of extra feds his way. "And add a mealpac to the program." With the discount, I could actually afford to eat.

"Sure." Sloan reached under the counter, pulled out a keyrod and a mealpac, and slid both across the stained countertop. "Room 206. Knock first. I told your roommate he'd probably be having company, but you don't want to surprise a freespacer. He might cut you in two and regret it later." He snickered. "Or he might not even regret it."

"Worthless data, gladeye." As if I'd be stupid enough to burst in on *any* stranger. How did Sloan think I'd survived this long?

I turned toward the stairs, but Sloan wasn't finished. "Oh, one other thing, Kit."

I glanced back. "Yeah?"

"Someone else was asking for you. Not just a musician. *You*, specifically. Man in a weathercoat. Looked like a high-power meatman to me." He grinned. "Sleep well."

"Not after seeing those teeth," I shot at him.

But as I climbed the stairs, my gut clenched. I'd been approached by street-level meatmen before; I told them "no," and they lifted. But if one of the herd-owners had his eyes on me...

And the guy in the weathercoat had been asking about me the same day this freespacer showed up at Sloan's asking about musicians? As I reached the dim and grimy second-floor corridor, I could almost feel the jaws of some hidden trap closing on me. *Maybe I should take my chances on the street after all...*

But the window at the end of the hall lit up with lightning, thunder crashed and rumbled, and wind howled, and I shook my head. *I'm inside. I'm warm. I'm dry. And it could all be coincidence.* I'd just be careful. *Really* careful.

I found Room 206 and stopped outside the door, listening. There was plenty to hear elsewhere in the flophouse: a man and a woman screaming obscenities somewhere; the latest Sensation Single pounding from the next room down the hall. I grimaced; I hated that pre-packaged fluff. But I could hear nothing from Room 206. Was that a good sign or not?

I took a deep breath, then knocked.

"Who's there?" said a voice, and my eyes widened. Sloan had said the spacer was a man, but the voice was soft, high-pitched—like a woman's!

I grinned. *Things are looking up!* "Your roommate," I said.

"Come in," said the feminine voice.

I stuck the keyrod into its port and, as the door swung inward, stepped through—

—and then jumped back out again, tripping over my own feet and falling on my butt with a thud. I pushed myself backward, crablike, until my stringsynth case pressed hard against the wall.

Two purple eyes on moist reddish-orange tentacles slid around the edge of the door and focused on me. A third eye joined them. "Are you unhurt?" said the voice that had told me to enter.

I found my own voice. I also found I couldn't do much with it. "I—I—"

"My name is..." The creature made a noise like tearing metal. "In your words...Water that Falls from the Sky?"

"Rain?" I croaked. I resolved to kill Sloan.

"Yes, Rain! Like what it is doing outside." A fourth eye rounded the corner, and then the entire creature.

Picture a stalk like a plant's, reddish-orange and dotted with irregular patches of silver and gold. Give it four insect-like legs, positioned equidistantly around the stalk, so it can move instantly in any direction. Top the stalk, about four feet up, with eight writhing tentacles, four of which end in the purple eyes that had been the first thing I'd seen. Add a mouth at the tentacles' base and breathing slits in the stalk that slowly open and close with a wet sucking sound, and you have my roommate. "You're a hydra!"

"That is what your race calls us, yes." The alien sounded slightly miffed. "We would prefer you to call us..." It—I didn't know if it was male or female—shrieked something well above high C.

"Not since my voice changed," I muttered.

"What?"

"Uh—nothing." I remembered I was sitting on the floor and scrambled to my feet. Fat Sloan's floors were nothing you wanted to sit on for long—or short, for that matter. "I'm sorry I yelled. Fat Slo—uh, the man who runs this place told me I'd have a roommate, but he didn't tell me he'd be—uh, one of you."

"Ah. Well, certainly I have the advantage of you there, for I *did* expect that my roommate would be human." Although the hydra's voice had that odd, almost feminine timbre, its Fedspeech was easy to understand, perfectly unaccented. "Won't you come in?"

"Uh—yeah. I mean, thanks." Clutching my synth and my mealpac to my chest, I edged into the room. The hydra made room for me, but not very much, and I dreaded the thought of bumping up against one of its—

I jumped as it laid a tentacle on my arm. Its orange skin felt very warm and slightly moist. "Your pardon," the hydra said. "I believe it is a human custom to exchange names. I've told you mine; you are...?"

"I'm called Kit," I said, a little breathlessly.

"Kit? Do not humans usually have two names or more?"

"I don't." I looked around the dingy little room. There was only one bed, but the hydra wouldn't use one, anyway.

I hoped.

"Is that usual?" the hydra said.

I tossed my stringsynth case on the bed and sat down beside it, then undid the laces on my left boot, wriggling my toes and hearing squelching sounds as I did so. "Most people have an individual name and a family name, but I don't have a family. My parents abandoned me when I was a baby." I pulled off the boot with rather more force than was necessary. "The orphanage didn't give me a name, just an ID number. I was supposed to choose my own name when I was twelve, local. In the meantime, they called me by a 'pre-name'—Kit."

"But surely...I am not a good judge of human ages, but surely you are older than twelve now."

I attacked the right boot. "Yeah, I'm fifteen, local—something like sixteen or seventeen, in Earth years—but I left the orphanage when I was ten, and I've had other things to worry about. Kit's good enough."

The hydra—Rain—said nothing, though its tentacles continued to move slowly. They made me queasy, so I stood up and went to the wash basin in one corner of the room, where I dumped the water from my boots. The rough towel Fat Sloan provided wasn't all that clean, but it was dry. I took off my coat, vest and two shirts; hesitated, then shrugged, stripped off the rest of my wet clothes and began rubbing myself dry. Being naked in front of a stranger hardly seemed to matter when it was a multi-tentacled alien who wasn't wearing any clothes itself. (And yet, I still didn't know if it was male or female—how could you tell?)

Rain spoke up again abruptly. "What is in this?" In the cracked mirror I saw the hydra lay one tentacle on my synth case.

"It's a stringsynth," I said. "A musical instrument." I towelled my tangled hair furiously. "I'm a street musician."

"A musician! A human musician!" All four of Rain's eyes focused on me suddenly. "I have been hoping to meet one! I am honoured!"

I wrapped the towel around my waist. "Well, that's a first." *Great. I finally get a groupie, and it's an alien.*

"Musicians have great prestige in our society." Rain caressed the synth's case. "And we admire human musicians especially. Your vocal apparatus is limited, but you create melodies we have never dreamed of—and your harmonies...! I am honoured, indeed."

I shook my head. "I'm just a streetkid with a beat-up old stringsynth. You've got nothing to learn from me."

"You are wrong, Kit. I have already learned much from you. I will choose to keep much of it."

Whatever *that* meant. "So, you know who I am. What about you?"

"What would you like to know?"

I reached for the mealpac and pulled its tab; the rich, nose-stinging odour of peppered greenfish steamed out of it, making my mouth water. "Well, first of all...if you don't mind my asking...are you male or female?"

His tentacles waved. "You really can't tell?"

"No."

"I am currently male."

"Currently?"

"We cycle among three sexes as we age. All hydras you see in Earth space are male. Neither our gender-neutral younglings nor our much-honoured female elders leave the planet."

Okay, then. At least I'll know next time I meet a hydra. I dug into the stew. "And what are you doing in Sloan's flophouse?"

"Flophouse?" Its—no, *his*, at least for now—tentacles waved. "What is—?"

"Hotel." I gestured at the yellowing walls with my spoon. "This place."

"It is as I told Mr. Sloan: I am a spacer, but I am between berths. I came here to enjoy new experiences."

I'd just taken another mouthful of stew, and I almost choked on it. "You mean you're here—in Fat Sloan's—as a *tourist*?"

"I believe that would be an accurate—do you need assistance?"

I swallowed before I gagged on laughter and fish broth. "No, no, I'm fine. Rain, if you want new experiences, stick with me. I'll show you a side of Fistfight City you can bet your—uh—bottom you've never seen before."

"Thank you!" Rain crowed. "I am in your debt, Kit. Will you also play some of your music for me?"

"Count on it."

Thunder shook the room and the wind shrieked through a crack in the window, but I was warm, dry, and eating. In my life, I'd learned not to ask for more than that.

Of course, as my roommate proved, sometimes we get things we don't ask for.

2

THE MAN IN THE WEATHERCOAT

RAIN ASKED SO many questions I thought he'd never let me sleep, but around midnight, he suddenly quit talking, in the middle of a sentence. That would have been great, except he didn't exactly fall silent; instead, he began to make a faint keening sound, like the wind, only higher-pitched and more constant. "Orbital," I muttered. If the pillow had smelled fresher, I'd have clamped it over my head. "Roomies with a snoring alien."

The sound kept on. I opened my eyes and looked at Rain in the uncertain light that spilled from the flashing red holosign of the tavern across the road. He had pulled all his tentacles into a tight ball atop his stalk, which pulsed slowly. I swallowed. I'd seen just about everything on the streets of Fistfight City, and never had a nightmare, but sharing a room with *that* just might manage it. Especially if he kept up that awful noise...

He did. But nothing else happened, and you can get used to any kind of noise if you hear it long enough—something I always figured explained the success of the Sensation Singles. Anyway, it had been a long day, and the bed, even if not particularly clean, was comfortable. Sometime while I was telling myself I'd be lying awake all night, I closed my eyes, and when I opened them again, sunlight on the puddle that had collected underneath the window cast rippling reflections on the walls.

Then I sat up and stared around the room. The rain that had fallen overnight had moved on. So, it appeared, had the Rain I'd shared my room with. There was no sign he'd ever been there.

Maybe I'd dreamed him.

Maybe I'd dreamed the man in the weathercoat, too. I hoped so.

My stomach growled, and I picked up the empty mealpac. I should have saved half of it for breakfast. Now I'd have to start the day hungry. Nothing new there, but not my first choice...

The door banged open and I scrambled back into the corner, grabbing the pillow to cover myself. The meatman? No, not unless he'd grown some more arms...

"Rain? Is that you?" As soon as I asked the question I felt stupid; what other four-eyed tentacled orange monster would be barging into my room first thing in the morning?

"Affirmative, it is I!" he chortled in that peculiar male/female voice. "I bring food!"

"Food?" I sat up straighter. "What kind of food?"

"I asked the tavern-woman across the street for food-which-you-eat-in-the-morning—"

"Breakfast."

"—breakfast, yes, and she gave me this." From somewhere he produced a mealpac twice the size of the one I'd gotten from Fat Sloan, and dropped it onto the pillow I held on my lap.

Mouthwatering steam filled the room as I tore back the cover. A redcheese and findel-egg omelette! I hadn't eaten anything that good in—I couldn't remember. Forever, maybe. It even came with a fork! I'd gulped half the contents before I remembered what passed for my manners. "Uh, Rain, did you want some?"

He made a choking noise that it took me a moment to recognize as laughter. "No, thank you. I ate only nine days ago."

"Oh." I didn't try to change his mind. Within minutes I swallowed the last tangy bite and sat back with a sigh.

All four of Rain's eyes watched me avidly. "Now will you go out on the street and sing?"

I sighed again. "What I'd really like to do is go back to sleep...but I won't!" I added hurriedly as Rain's tentacles writhed. "Fat Sloan will be kicking people out in a few minutes, anyway—except for the crashed-out flashmen. Those, he'll just leave where they are, and charge them for a second night." I got up, tossed the pillow aside, and padded naked to the sink. There was a shower down the hall, but you never knew who you'd meet in there. I'd have to settle for a wet washrag and some of Fat Sloan's gritty soap.

"I have heard of these 'flashmen,'" said Rain. "They are humans who have become addicted to a chemical substance, yes?"

I ran water on the rag, then wet the soap. "Yeah, flash."

"And why do they take this substance?"

"To escape."

"Escape? Escape what?"

"Their lives. Places like this." I sniffed at the washrag. Either it or the soap smelled rancid. I settled for splashing water over myself, then rubbing down with the towel.

"But even after they take it, they are still here."

"Not in their heads." I tapped my forehead. "Up here, they're somewhere else—even some*one* else. Plus, it makes you feel really strong and fast, like you could do anything."

"You have tried it?"

I tossed the towel aside and reached for my clothes—still damp, but all I had. "No. But I've heard." And some nights, I'd been tempted. I pulled on my thin, ragged underwear, then forced my legs into my still-damp blackjeans.

"Where do these 'flashmen' get this substance?"

"Just about anywhere," I said, zipping up. "There's a dealer on every block. Fat Sloan, for example."

"And where do *they* get it?"

My shirt, also considerably short of perfectly dry, felt like a sheet of ice on my back. "How should I know?" I snapped. "You sure do ask a lot of questions!"

"I wish to learn about your culture," said Rain. "That is why I am here. These things I am learning from you were not included in the data on Murdoch IV contained in the ship's computer."

"Yeah?" I reached for my socks. "Well, I don't know much about the rest of the planet, but if you want data about its lovely capital city, I know stuff that will slag your hardware." I shoved my feet into my boots, then got up, pulled on my jacket, slapped my old hat on my head, and grabbed the stringsynth. "Let's lift for the street, gladeye!"

"Gladeye?"

I sighed. "That's street slang for friend—you know, I see you, I feel glad, so 'gladeye.'"

Rain's eyes stacked up one above the other above the other above the other. "I have not heard this! My knowledge of your language is incomplete."

"No," I said. "You speak standard Fedspeech very well. But individual groups—like streetkids—speak variations of it."

He sidled closer, staring so intently with all four purple eyes that I took a step back. (You haven't really been stared at 'til you've been stared at by a hydra.) "Your pattern of speech is inconsistent," he said. "Sometimes you speak 'standard' speech and sometimes this 'slang.' I do not understand."

"I don't plan to be a streetslug all my life," I said. "Whenever I've got a few extra feds I plug the self-teachers at Data Central." I grinned at him and put on the clipped accent of the Planetary Governor. "I am perfectly capable of speaking standard Fedspeech; however, such a mode of communication would not serve me well among my peers in the underprivileged class."

Rain wriggled his eyes. "Most intriguing! I will retain it."

I laughed. "Orbital, gladeye. Let's lift!"

"Slang," he said joyfully. "Let's lift!"

I intended to go back to the tube station—morning rush hour was usually good for a couple of feds—but Rain turned to the right when I turned left, then stopped, his eyes swivelling around to stare at me. "You are not going to the spaceport?"

"Why should I?" I asked suspiciously.

"A big passenger liner lands this morning. Tourists, I think you call them? Are not such people your ideal audience?"

He was right, but I hesitated. The port was the Ice Boys'

orbit and the last time I'd hit it they'd half-strangled me with my own stringsynth strap.

I gave Rain a measuring look. On the other hand, last time I hadn't had an orange octopus sidekick. Besides, I could use the feds—and though I hated to admit it, the man in the weather-coat had spooked me. He wouldn't look for me in the Port because I hadn't been there in months.

"Orbital, gladeye," I said. "Program accepted. Let's lift!"

At the port, nobody tried to strangle me. But nobody threw money in my case, either, because the tourists were fresh off some planet even further out of the galactic cultural main-stream than Murdoch IV (which I should have guessed from the fact they'd come to Fistfight City to "see the sights," since there weren't any) and had never seen a hydra. Instead of listening to me, they all clustered around Rain, staring. He stared back, sometimes at four different people at once. For all his "I am honoured" talk, he didn't seem to be paying much attention to me. I broke off in the middle of a raunchy Belvederian folksong and glared at him. "You're negativizing my audience, Rain."

"Hey, it's smooth, gladeye," he said. "I'll lift."

Which he did. Trouble was, he took the people with him. After two hours I'd collected less than the price of even one of Fat Sloan's measly mealpacs. I frowned at Rain and the crowd around him. Maybe I could hide him in the men's room and charge admission. *See the incredible octoman! One fed a head...*

"Hey, flashmates. Scan who's back in our orbit."

Uh-oh. Little problem I hadn't considered with having Rain move off. I turned slowly. "What's powering, Dry Ice?"

He and three other Ice Boys were leaning against two of the mirrored pillars that dotted the terminal lobby. Since they wore mirrorcloth themselves, the effect was unsettling—as intended. Not that it took special effects to unsettle me. I hadn't forgotten what Dry Ice had promised to do to me the next time he caught me in the Port. It involved the monomolecular forceblades all the Ice Boys carried and the most sensitive parts of my anatomy. I hoped Dry Ice didn't remember as well as I did.

No such luck. He flicked his right hand and a black hilt sprang into his palm from beneath his mirrorcloth sleeve. A faint, whispering hum told me the deadly, invisible blade was active. I slowly knelt, put the stringsynth into its case, then stood and slung the case over my shoulder, keeping my eyes on him the whole time. "Power down, Dry Ice. It's smooth. I'm lifting."

"You missed the launch window, gladeye." Dry Ice stepped toward me. The whites of his narrowed eyes showed blue-grey —the sign of a long-time flash-user. His brain was in permanent overdrive now, craving new sensations—like the sensation of slicing bits off my quivering body. See, that was a side effect of flash I hadn't mentioned to Rain: it could turn even kind and gentle people into dangerous, violent psychopaths—and Dry Ice had *never* been either kind or gentle.

He showed his teeth. "You've crashed our orbit for the last time." His flashmates fanned out, surrounding me. I looked back at Rain; not a single eye pointed in my direction. I tensed, ready to run, though I knew from bitter experience the Ice Boys were faster—but, suddenly, Dry Ice stopped his advance. The hum of his forceblade stopped and the hilt snapped back beneath his sleeve. "Hey, it's smooth, gladeye. It's smooth!"

I turned, following his gaze. At the top of the escalator stood the man in the long black weathercoat. "Lift," he told Dry Ice and his boys, and they lifted, though not without black looks over their shoulders, whether at me or the man in the weathercoat, I couldn't tell.

I watched warily as the stranger descended to my level "You're Kit?" he said as he reached me.

"Information's economic, gladeye. Freeware's a myth."

"Cut the slang. I know you can talk standard Fedspeech."

"Yeah?" I didn't like this at all. He knew too much about me, while I knew nothing about him—except that I had something he wanted. I was behind in the game and didn't even know the rules, much less the stakes.

"Yeah." He glanced at Rain, who apparently hadn't noticed the Ice Boys at all—or hadn't cared.

Just because we slept in the same space doesn't make us friends, I reminded myself, *or I'd have a lot more friends than I do.*

As if reading my thoughts, the stranger said, "Saw you come in with the hydra. Friend of yours?"

"Acquaintance."

"Interesting acquaintance for a streetslug."

"He likes music."

"That a fact?" The man's teeth flashed white. "So do I." He nodded toward Rain. "Let's go see if he likes *yours.*"

"I'm lifting," I said. "Ice Boys come back, I'm protein."

"Ice Boys won't bother you while you're with me."

That wasn't reassuring. Who *was* this guy? Still, I took his unspoken point: the Ice Boys wouldn't bother me while I was with him, but when I *wasn't* with him anymore... "So, let's go talk to my good friend Rain," I said.

"Good idea," said the man. Weathercoat swirling, he strode to where Rain held court. Nobody stared at Rain for long, not once he started staring back, but new people kept emerging from Customs. In the crowd, I caught a glimpse of a kid I knew. He'd probably had a very profitable morning, what with all those tourists too interested in the alien to pay any attention to their pockets.

The man in the weathercoat held up a flat silver box and a nerve-grating screech assaulted my ears. Rain's eyes whirled to face us. He screeched back.

The man bowed to him. "I regret I cannot further converse in your tongue. Only the greeting-of-one-for-a-stranger is programmed into my autotranslator."

"Regret nothing," said Rain. "It was a pleasure to hear our language spoken unexpectedly. I shall retain it."

"I am honoured." The man straightened. "I am called Qualls. You are Rain?"

"I am..." He shrieked, and I winced. "But 'Rain' is acceptable." His eyes rearranged themselves. "I have memory of you, Qualls. You were on the ship that brought me here five days ago."

"I am honoured my memory was retained."

Rain aimed an eye at me. "You are a friend of my young gladeye Kit?"

"More of an admirer," Qualls said. "I have been watching him since I arrived."

"You've been *what?*" I exploded.

"Watching you. I've been very impressed."

"I'm nobody's meat!"

"I'm not a meatman." He turned back toward Rain. "You are interested in human music, Rain. I would value your opinion."

"Kit has great talent," Rain said instantly. "Untrained and raw, but very promising. I will retain much of what I heard."

Qualls bowed. "Thank you. You confirm my own opinion."

I stared at both of them. "What's going on?"

Qualls held out a glowing rectangle—a holocard. I glanced at it. Beside the three-dimensional image of his face floated six words that sparkled like diamonds: "Samuel Qualls. Talent Scout. Sensation Singles."

I gaped at him. He smiled. "Kit," he said, "I'm going to make you a star."

3

FROM THE STREET TO THE STARS

QUALLS TOOK ME TO LUNCH, upstairs in a fancy restaurant in a part of the spaceport I didn't even know existed. He invited Rain along, too, and the hydra accepted eagerly, although the waiter who greeted us didn't look too happy about the alien's presence. Neither did the half-dozen patrons whose variously horrified or disgusted faces I glimpsed among the ferns and fountains that mostly hid the tables and chairs. But Rain, as far as I could tell (not very far, I admit), was unperturbed. His eyestalks practically tied themselves in knots as he ogled everything, and he chirped musically to himself all the while.

The waiter showed us to a table by a window overlooking the spaceport. Close to the terminal, the bulbous grey shapes of four commercial passenger ships loomed over the scurrying vehicles that serviced them. Off at the edge of the field, large freighters crouched like distant thunderclouds. But my eyes went immediately to a sleek and silvery yacht that gleamed

22

among the others like a silver knife carelessly tossed among old spoons.

"Like it?" Qualls asked.

Instantly on guard, I put on my best bored-stiff face and turned my back on the window. "It's a ship. So what? You own it, meatman?"

His eyes narrowed. "I told you, I'm not a meatman."

"Yeah?" I flicked his card onto the table. "You buy and sell people. What do you call it?"

Rain had two eyes on me and two eyes on Qualls. I wondered if he could feel the tension between us—or understand it. So, Qualls said he would make me a star. Well, I wasn't buying real estate on Earth just yet. I trusted myself—no one else. Especially not someone who would treat streetslime to a meal in a restaurant like this.

If I even got the meal. I had my doubts.

But Qualls surprised me by laughing. "Maybe you have a point, Kit. Enough business for now. Are you hungry?"

He knew I was hungry. But I shrugged. "Not much."

"Well, I insist you try something. This restaurant has surprisingly good food, considering the location." I wondered if he meant the spaceport or the planet. "Waiter!"

He ordered dishes I'd never heard of, and they came in minutes. Qualls only picked at a small plate of purple roots—or were they worms?—but both he and Rain watched as I devoured everything the waiter set in front of me. Pride's all very well, but I'd never seen a meal like that in my life and figured I might never see one again. Calories are calories. I ate.

At last, too full to eat any more—a new sensation I liked

very much—I sat back and stared at Qualls. He gazed stolidly back. "Well?" I said.

"Well?"

"Well, what is it you want? And don't feed me more biowaste about making me a star."

"No waste." He pointed to his card. "I am what that says I am—a talent scout for Sensation Singles, Inc."

"He speaks the truth, Kit," said Rain.

"How would you know?" I snapped.

"I spoke to him on the ship coming in."

"He could have been lying to you, too."

Rain goggled at me with all four eyes. "What would he gain by that?"

The thought occurred to me that they had *both* lied, to set me up, but even I wasn't that paranoid. "Then why me? Why here?"

"Sensation Singles have to come from somewhere," said Qualls. "Very specific somewheres, actually. Each one is carefully chosen from a particular socio-economic and planetary background. Our computer projections indicate it's time for a tough, street-smart male from this part of the galaxy. Fistfight City's streets are the meanest in Confederation. Drug trafficking, prostitution, cyberjacking, bodypart snatching—Fistfight City has it all. That makes it perfect." He shrugged. "The choice of you specifically? Coincidence. I heard you outside my hotel the day I arrived. Musical ability isn't absolutely necessary, but it's nice when we can find it, and I'm sure you can learn the dance steps."

"You're saying you're going to 'make me a star' because I was in the right place at the right time—pure luck?"

"Pure luck."

"Huh." Good luck and I weren't really on speaking terms—but it was easier to believe I'd lucked out than that some stranger had crossed the galaxy to find me. "So, what's in it for me?"

Qualls smiled. "Fame and money."

"As a Sensation Single? I'll be forgotten in a year."

"Absolutely. But the money will last a lot longer." He leaned forward, folding his arms on the table. "What do you want, Kit?"

"Enough food to eat. A warm, dry place to sleep."

"And after that?"

"I've never even gotten that, yet."

"Forget food and shelter. You'll have enough money to do anything you want. So, what will you spend it on?"

I laughed. "Myself." I glanced out the window. "Maybe I'll buy a yacht."

"No need."

"What?"

"You've already got one." He nodded at the gleaming silver ship. "That's *The Bullet*. For the express use of Andy Nebula."

"Andy *who*?"

"Andy Nebula. The next Sensation Single." Qualls cocked his head and one corner of his mouth quirked upward. "You?"

I stared out at the yacht. Money, fame, a chance to leave Fistfight City...and though I wasn't about to tell Qualls, I did dream of something more than being warm and fed. I dreamed of writing, performing, and recording my own music, of making some kind of permanent mark. With money, even that might be possible.

I let the last of my suspicions go. "Me," I said.

"Orbital, gladeye!" shrieked Rain at a pitch about an octave above high C. The window vibrated dangerously.

"Uh, thanks," I said, removing my hands from my ears, wondering what he was so happy about. Nobody had offered to make *him* a star—not surprising, with a voice like that.

He backed away from the table. "I'll leave you to your business discussions," he said at a more normal pitch. "I am pleased, gladeye Kit, to see my new friend honoured in this way. I look forward to your performances." He scuttled off.

"Thanks," I said again, to empty air.

Qualls leaned back in his chair. "First things first." He pulled something the size of a sugar cube out of his coat pocket, put it on the table, and pressed his thumb to it. A holoscreen popped up between us, filled with text. "This is our standard contract." He poked his finger into it; the first paragraph enlarged. "Let me just go over a few points with you..."

———

AND SO IT BEGAN. Almost like in my official biography. Within a day I had new clothes, a new name, a new hairstyle, and an extremely comfortable apartment in a self-contained module aboard *The Bullet*. It turned out the yacht, which was much larger than it had appeared from the restaurant, also featured a full-sized stage, a full stage crew (humans *and* robots), and enough dancebots and holoprojectors to recreate everything choreographed since the first caveman pranced around a campfire.

Two days after I signed Qualls's contract, we lifted from Fistfight City. I hardly noticed, since I was trying to push my sweating and aching body through my second dance lesson at the time.

Rehearsal followed rehearsal. The dance steps came more easily. I quit kicking the lightweight dancebots across the stage accidentally or stumbling through the holo-projected "walls" of the set. My personal Sensation Single, "From the Street to the Stars," I learned in a single day—not much of a feat, since it was a computer-crafted ear-worm designed to not just stick in your head but follow you around for days like a lost puppy. I learned a handful of companion pieces, too, forgettable fluff that existed only to flesh out a full-length concert. I asked if I could perform one of my own songs, but apparently that was forbidden by the contract I'd signed (Qualls hadn't pointed out *that* paragraph).

I rehearsed all day, every day, and well into every night—not that those terms mean much on a spaceship. In the meantime, the Sensation Singles publicity machine went into high gear. I was photographed, holographed, and made into an animated doll; the celebrity-hungry press on all seventy-nine Confederated Worlds received my largely fictitious biography; when deemed ready, I recorded my Single; sometime later, I danced through the entire extended version of the song (exactly twenty-two minutes) under the scrutiny of both flatscreen and holovid cameras; two weeks after that, my song and video hit the airwaves; and three days later, I debuted in the Big Wheel, a giant amusement satellite orbiting Decca VI, to 60,000 screaming teenagers, each of whom had been carefully chosen to look good on the *Andy Nebula Live* special that went out Confederation-wide the very next day.

I'd never performed for more than a dozen people at a time

in my life, but as the concert approached I felt no nervousness, only exhilaration. I'd rehearsed to the point I could do "From the Street to the Stars" and all the other songs in my sleep—and often did, in my dreams. And the set blew me away. I could have sworn, the first time they turned on the holos and I stepped on stage, that I was back in the alleys of Fistfight City—except these alleys looked even darker and more dangerous. The dance moves, stylized from police vid of gang fights, supported a basic storyline of boy (me) meets girl, boy loses girl to flash-gang leader, boy bravely fights gang leader and wins, boy and girl ride off into sunset. (It would have been a lot more fun if the "girl" had been real instead of a dancebot, though.)

I stood in the wings, listening to the crowd chant, "An-*dy*, An-*dy*, An-*dy*," and felt their energy pour over me and into me like a breaking wave. "Better get out there before they tear the satellite apart," Marcel, the stage manager, said in my earplug. A pounding drumbeat began, the roar of the crowd rose to an incredible volume—and then the set lit up, the stringsynths rasped through the blistering riff that opened the piece, and I dashed out on stage.

I couldn't see a thing through the lights and the holowalls and everything else, but I could sense every individual in that vast crowd screaming my made-up name. I rode their energy and danced and sang like I never had before, even for the vid. I wasn't streetslime anymore—no way. At the climax, I smashed the "gang leader" dancebot out of my way with a spinning, leaping kick, and thought, *Suck vacuum, Dry Ice!* Every screaming kid out there knew, *knew* I was the greatest thing they had ever seen, and in that moment, I knew it, too—and I liked it. I liked it a lot.

Qualls had kept his word. I was a star.

I powered my way through the remaining songs in set-list, ending with a reprise of the chorus of "From the Street to the Stars," the whole crowd singing along. When it was over, I stood backstage, panting, mirrorcloth tights soaked with sweat, and thought I heard, in the blood pounding in my ears, words of caution. *It won't last...it can't last...* But as I ran onstage again to accept the wild, screaming, standing ovation, as I watched blue sparks crackling around the hands of girls braving the sting of the static fields to get as close to me as possible, I forgot that warning voice. *This* was what I was meant for.

Kit, the ragged streetkid from Fistfight City, was gone for good. He'd been replaced by an interstellar superstar:

Andy Nebula!

4

PARIS PARADISE

SIX MONTHS PASSED in a blur of performances, interviews, rehearsals, and travel, but every night I felt that same surge of exhilaration just before I went on, as the crowd thundered, the synths built the pounding backbeat, the lasers flashed through the smoke, and the dancebots whirled. I was the detonator of a bomb; when I stepped on stage, things exploded.

At the end of the six months, we were on Carstair's Folly, the fourteenth stop in my triumphant tour of the Pleasure Planets. I stood in the wings in my mirrorcloth skintights until the crowd was threatening to tear down the soaring gossamer roof of the acoustic tent, then I gave the signal, the computer shouted, "Ladies and gentleman—Andy Nebula!", and I burst onto the stage and ripped into my sizzling opening dance, while the dancebots fell back in shock and phantom stars exploded overhead.

We had 125,000 people there that night and I felt good as I

finished my bows and made my exit, the crowd still chanting, "An-*dy*! An-*dy*! An-*dy*!"

Qualls waited backstage; unusual, but not *that* unusual. "Hey, Qualls," I shouted above the crowd noise. "They still love me."

"Come in here a minute, Kit."

I followed him into his soundproof office, and he pointed me to the formchair across from his silver-topped desk. I sat down gingerly—I hate the way those things flow to conform to my butt. "What's powering, manager-man?"

"Cut the slang, Kit."

"Hey, that's my homebabble, glad—"

"I said *cut it!*"

I cut it. "What's wrong?"

He sat down and pulled a whirligig bottle from a drawer, along with two glasses. He filled them both and pushed one to me. I took it, but my stomach fluttered; Qualls never risked heat from the local 'forcers, and on Carstair's Folly legal drinking age was nineteen standard Earth years, and I was (by my best estimate) still only seventeen. Here, serving an intoxicant to a minor, even an intoxicant as weak as whirligig, could land you in jail. Still, the cold fizzy liquid felt great going down. I drank half of it in a gulp, burped, then lowered my glass to see Qualls staring moodily into his own. "Well?" I said.

"You saw the crowd tonight, Kit."

"Looked good. The tent was full."

"Tents are always full, Kit...because you can move the walls."

I stared at him. "What?"

"Capacity is 200,000. We sold two-thirds of that. You weren't a sellout, Kit."

The fluttery feeling in my stomach grew. I guzzled more whirligig, but the fluttering didn't go away. I wiped my mouth with the back of my hand and set down the glass with a thump. "That's...what? 130,000 tickets? More than twice the size of the crowd at my debut. At a hundred feds apiece, that's still not exactly biowaste!"

"Maybe. But it's the first time Andy Nebula hasn't sold out."

"The next planet—"

"Ticket sales are slow. I just got a call from Mr. Korpov."

I wondered if I could get Qualls to serve me something stronger than whirligig. Korpov was the CEO of Sensation Singles, Inc. "He's fading me out?"

"Not yet. You've got four more concerts, no matter what. But if you're not back to sell-outs by that fourth gig..."

"Yeah, I know." I'd *always* known. None of this could last. Sensation Singles were like non-repeating comets; one blaze of glory, then cold oblivion for eternity. "The crowds will come back, Qualls. I'm sure of it."

"Right, Kit." He drained his whirligig in four gulps. "You'd better go get cleaned up. They'll be moving your dressing room back to the ship in about an hour. We lift tonight."

I stood up, the formchair releasing me reluctantly, and handed him my glass. "I'm vapour, gladeye." My usual post-concert bubbly feeling had gone thoroughly flat, whirligig notwithstanding. I trudged to my dressing room in a mood as black as the shadows that filled the backstage corridors.

As I neared my dressing-room door, one of those shadows moved.

I froze, heart racing. In my experience, moving shadows were bad news. The last moving shadow I'd seen, in a Fistfight City alley not far from Fat Sloan's, had been armed with a very nasty zapclub and an even nastier temperament. Fortunately, I was so obviously streetslime he hadn't bothered with me. But I wasn't streetslime anymore, I was a superstar, and prime fodder for—

"Got you!" said the shadow.

"What?" I looked frantically around for security. What did we pay them for, anyway?

"They got you, got you, got you!" The shadow moved forward, and a red bulbous nose appeared in the light, followed by squinting, puffy eyes, and bared, yellowing teeth.

"Who got me?" I backed up against the wall. In the Fistfight City alley I'd at least had my battered old stringsynth to use as a club or shield (which was one reason it was so battered), but now I had nothing but my personality and my mirrorcloth, and I didn't think either would dazzle this madman.

"*They* got you!" He waved toward the stage. "The sssss...sssss..." Whatever word he wanted wouldn't come. Face contorted, he slammed his fist against the wall so hard I thought I heard a bone break. I jumped, and he shouted in my face, "Got you like they got me like they got her like they got we —we've all been got, got, got, only—" He broke off suddenly, stared up and down the corridor, then leaned in close. His breath reeked of something considerably stronger than whirligig. "I escaped."

"Goo—good for you."

"You can, too." For the first time his eyes opened wide, and I shivered. The whites were blue-grey, even darker than his blue irises. He was a flashman, and if he was flashing now, he could tear me into little pieces with his bare hands.

It seemed like a good reason to be friendly. "Uh...how?"

He looked at me like *I* was crazy. "Run!" he whispered, then screamed, "Run! Run! Run!"

Footsteps, at last, clattered down the corridor. "Andy?"

"Marcel!" I yelled. "Help!"

The flashman glared at me, pulled back his fist as if he were going to punch me, then said calmly, "Think about it," and turned and ran—straight into the arms of a burly security guard. "Let me go!" he shouted. "I'm Paris Paradise! They're waiting for me on—" He slumped suddenly, head lolling. Marcel's grey-bearded face appeared behind the security man's bulk.

"Did you trank him?" Marcel asked.

"Didn't have to," the guard grunted as he heaved the flashman over his shoulder. "I think he just crashed on his own. I'm sorry, Mr. Roy. I don't know how he got past us."

"Figure it out soon or you'll be looking for a new job," Marcel snapped. "Get him out of here." He came over to where I leaned against the wall. "Are you all right, Kit?"

"Sure," I said. "He didn't do anything except talk." I straightened, then casually leaned against the wall again. My legs weren't quite ready to move me yet.

"I've got to talk to Qualls," Marcel muttered. He hurried back up the corridor, while I stumbled the last few metres to my dressing room. I closed the door, then sat on the bed, looked at my trembling hands, and clenched them into fists.

"I'm getting soft," I muttered. "I've been through a lot

worse." But that was in Fistfight City. In my new life, things like this weren't supposed to happen.

Good thing my fans will never know about it. With my fake hero-of-the-streets image, they'd never understand why I hadn't simply knocked him down and dragged him off to security myself...especially since they were mostly teenage girls with well-to-do parents and nice safe homes. Most of them had probably never even heard of flash. I wished *I* hadn't.

They'd never understand what it had *really* been like on the streets, just trying to survive. There had even been times when, if the orphanage would have taken me back, I'd have gladly put up with any kind of abuse just to be warm and fed. And for all my pride at never selling myself to a meatman, I'd been a lot closer to it than I wanted to admit, more times than I liked to remember. Street life was almost no life at all, and I had no wish to go back to it—or to Fistfight City. The money I'd earned would keep me off the streets, but it wouldn't keep me out of Fistfight City, if what Qualls said about ticket sales was true. That's where my contract specified I had to eventually be returned, since the law assumed minors should be sent "home."

I looked around the dressing room. Although it was one big open space, except for the bathroom, it was the nicest place I'd ever lived. My bed was to my left, a wardrobe space behind closed doors to my right. The bathroom was straight ahead. On the other side of the bed, there was a sitting area, with a loveseat and a couple of armchairs clustered around a black-topped coffee table, facing a giant vidscreen, and a small desk with a computer terminal. The far end of the module was a miniature kitchen, complete with cooker and cooler and dish-cleanser, and a small, round dining table with two chairs. Everything was black, silver, grey, or white: white walls, black-and-white furniture, grey carpet, silver appliances. *This* was home, and I didn't want to give it up. Maybe if we boosted promotion...

Who was I kidding? You couldn't possibly boost promotion above the Sensation Singles Inc.'s normal hysterical level.

My terminal beeped, announcing a message. Probably the local media, and I wasn't in the mood. I stripped out of my mirrortights and stepped into the shower, thinking about the Ice Boys as I soaped away sweat. They'd had the same grey-blue eyes as the old flashman. Some of the ones who'd cornered me in the spaceport six months ago were probably dead by now; a lot of people couldn't handle flash—they'd OD within a couple of months. But others went on for years and years, getting stronger and nastier and crazier. I had an uncomfortable feeling Dry Ice might be one of those. I wondered if he knew where I'd gone.

I stepped out of the shower. Brown eyes stared back at me from the mirror. My face and body were a little more filled out than they had been that day in the Fistfight City spaceport, but otherwise I looked the same—same shaggy black hair, same less-than-perfect nose, broken by "accident" after I spilled a bowl of soup in the orphanage. My disreputable appearance had happened to mesh perfectly with the image Sensation Singles, Inc., had cultivated for me, so I'd escaped plastic surgery. Which meant that, yeah, Dry Ice would know what had become of me —hanging around the Port, he could hardly have avoided my video blaring from holoprojectors and flatscreens everywhere.

I dried off and padded back into my dressing room, tossing the towel on the bed. I glanced at the beeping terminal, decided

I couldn't keep ignoring it, and tapped RECEIVE. Blue letters scrolled across the screen. "Again you make pleasant memories I shall retain, gladeye. Your ex-roomie, Rain."

I laughed. I should have known. I'd already had half a dozen similar messages from Rain, in the most unexpected places, but I'd never seen him in person. I'd pretty well decided he wasn't actually at the concerts—he was sending the messages from off-planet. If he really were attending the concerts, why didn't he ever pop backstage to see me? If an old flashman could get through Security, surely a hydra could...

Still, I felt better. At least I had one fan left.

I cleared the screen, then crossed the room to my closet. Before I reached it, someone knocked. "Who is it?" I called.

No answer, but I heard the latch click open. "Wait a minute!" I yelled, and grabbed the towel from the bed, getting it in front of me just as the door swung open and—

I stared in astonishment. "Who are *you*?"

5

THE GIRL IN THE DRESSING ROOM

I HAD a quick impression of wide, bright-blue eyes and short black hair, and then my unexpected visitor squealed, almost as loud as a hydra. After a painful few seconds her squeal resolved into words. "You're Andy Nebula!"

"In the flesh," I said, extremely aware that all that was between me and her was the not-as-big-as-I-would-have-liked towel in my strategically placed hand. I quickly wrapped it around my waist.

The emitter of the squeal was a girl a standard year or two younger than me. She wore a glittergold blouse emblazoned with a half-holo of my face, which winked at me whenever she shifted position. Below that were mirrorcloth tights, and below that transparent platform shoes that made her look like they she was floating barefoot ten centimetres above the floor. Her toenails were painted silver. "I'm sorry, I didn't—I mean, I knocked first and—"

"Never mind." At least she didn't have a camera...not one

big enough for me to see, anyway, although of course there could be a camdot hiding somewhere among the sequins of that glittering blouse. *I'm going to make Marcel fire our security team. First a flashman, and now a groupie?* Fans were *never* supposed to see Sensation Singles in unscripted situations. They might realize we were ordinary human beings, and we couldn't have that, could we?

Well, she could see *I* was an ordinary human being, all right, and getting to be a chilly one, because there was a cold draft blowing in from the corridor. "Look, you're not supposed to be here," I said. *You'll have to leave,* I intended to add, but—

"I know!" she said breathlessly, ducking inside and closing the door behind her. "Isn't it wonderful? Just like in your vid, when Bloodstone tells you to get off the planet and instead you sneak into their hideout and Rocket Rick sees you and says—"

"'You're not supposed to be here,'" I finished for her. "Yeah, I know, but you're *really* not supposed to be here. You'll get in trouble."

"It's worth it to see you!"

I sighed. "All right, great, anything for a true fan, but would you mind doing me a favour?"

"Anything," she breathed.

"Turn around so I can get dressed?"

"Oh!" She blushed, and quickly faced the wall. "I've got my eyes closed, too!"

"Orbital." I dropped the towel and pulled on underwear and then the first outfit I could find—an all-black affair, synthileather pants and microfibre shirt. "All right, I'm decent."

She turned, then frowned. "That's not what Andy Nebula wears."

"I left Andy Nebula on stage." I grabbed a brush and quickly ran it through my wet hair. "Call me Kit."

"You mean—Andy Nebula's not your real name?"

She sounded so shocked I had to laugh. "'Fraid not." I tossed the brush aside, got some socks (also black) from the dresser, then sat down on the bed to pull them on, followed by my favourite pair of soft-soled boots. "Look, what's *your* name?"

"My name? You want to know *my* name?" You'd have thought I'd just handed her a million feds. "Meta."

"Well, Meta, I'm glad you like my Single, but if security finds you they're going to be very upset and they're going to ask you a lot of questions, not very gently, and then they're going to throw you out, even less gently. Plus, this whole dressing room is going to be sealed and moved to my ship in a few minutes. So, I really think you should get out however it was you got in—"

"It was easy," she said. "An old man came running out and all the Security people chased after him and I just walked in."

I groaned. "Great. I'm lucky a thousand fans didn't come into my room while I was naked."

"Oh, no, there was nobody else out there. Everyone knows you never see a Single by hanging around the stage door."

"Except you?"

"But that's different. I mean, *I'm* different. I mean, I like to try new things." She smiled shyly. "Just like you say in your song, you know, 'I don't follow the crowd/I shout it out loud/when they tell me to go/Gonna stay, don't you know?'"

I winced. She'd sung that last part. Sort of. "Well, you'd better get out of here now, and I mean it."

"All right." At the door, she stopped and looked back. "I'll see you again. Real soon."

"Oh, yeah?" If a million or two other kids felt the same way, Korpov might get off my back. "Great. I'll look for you in the crowd." As if I could pick out one face even if I wanted to.

She smiled and slipped out. I sat on the bed and stared at the closed door for a minute. I really should tell Marcel...but that might get Meta in trouble, and I didn't want that. I had to admire her guts. Not at all what I'd have expected from a Pleasure Planet brat.

So instead, I let it slide. No harm done. I got up again, secured the dressing room for transport, then walked back to the stage. Qualls's office had already been hauled away, and the stagebots had dismantled the projectors and lights, leaving only a scuffed black platform. The roof and walls of the tent sagged. Soon only the litter of discarded programs, snackpacs, and drink containers would be left, and a large vacant lot. Time to move on.

Marcel emerged from the wings. "Dressing room ready?"

"Yeah," I said. "And so am I." I walked over to him as he plugged his handcomp into the lead stagebot to activate its preflight routine. "I heard the flashman got away."

"Yeah," Marcel grunted. "But not far. Ran out in front a speeding wheeler. It wasn't pretty."

I felt a pang. "Poor old flashman."

"Not as old as you think." Marcel disconnected his handcomp from the 'bot, which rolled away to store itself for transport.

I stared at him. "What? Did you know him?"

"Of course not. All I meant was, flash burns people out."

"But—"

"Your transportation's waiting." He strode off. I stared after him for a moment, puzzled, then headed for the stage door.

I opened it to discover rain pounding the pavement. I could barely make out my private wheeler through the downpour: it was parked a good thirty metres away, blocked from coming any closer by the massive transport crawler whose crane was even then lifting my dressing room. I swore, then dashed into the storm, splashing through puddles, arriving at the little black two-seater soaked to the skin. I clambered into the passenger seat and took revenge by shaking my hair like a dog, spraying the blue interior. The driver, a Sensation Single Inc. employee I knew distantly, glared at me and pulled away from the curb way too fast, snapping my head back against the headrest. "Where'd you learn to drive?" I snarled.

"Same place you learned to sing, streetslime," he snapped.

I gaped at him. Sensation Single employees *never* spoke that way to performers; it could get them fired.

Yeah, it could, I thought nastily. I smiled. "Tired of your job?"

"Now, why should I be tired of chauffeuring an obnoxious brat?" He skidded around a corner so fast I banged hard against the door.

I straightened, rubbing my bruised elbow. "When Qualls hears about this—"

"At this point in your so-called career, kid, I'm more valuable to Mr. Qualls than you." He grinned at me—or at least bared his teeth. "You're the sixth little puffed-up no-talent brat I've chauffeured. You 'stars' come and go. I'm always here. So, shut your mouth and enjoy this fancy ride while you've still got it."

I wanted to knock that smirk from his face—but the scary

thing was, he could be right. So instead I shut up and turned toward the window, seething. Everybody thought I was heading for a crash-and-burn. Well, we'd see. There were still four confirmed shows. Ticket sales could still pick up and boost me back into orbit. *I'm going to be the first Sensation Single to keep the music going,* I thought—in which case vacuum-brain here would find himself driving garf-drawn carriages on Stimpson's Regret, and as everybody knows, nothing stinks worse than garf manure.

I slammed the door extra hard as I got out at the ship.

Each of the modules from backstage, including my dressing room, plugged neatly into *The Bullet*'s hold. Until my dressing room arrived I had no place to go, so I made my way to the passenger lounge to get something to eat and listen to someone else's music for a change.

Use of the lounge was restricted to me, Qualls, and VIP guests, so while I wasn't surprised to see Qualls there, I didn't expect to see a two-metre-tall, orange, tentacled alien enthusiastically downing something that bubbled and smoked like hydrochloric acid laced with iron filings. "Rain, old gladeye!" I shouted gleefully, rushing toward him.

Tentacles that felt like steel wire wrapped in thin, wet rubber lashed around my neck, arms, and legs, immobilizing me, then tightening until I could hardly breathe. Four purple eyes glared at me. "Or maybe not," I choked out.

Qualls chuckled. "Never startle a hydra, Andy."

"Good—urk!—advice."

The hydra released me. I managed a smile. Qualls had called me "Andy," which meant this was business. I wished he'd warned me, not only because it would have saved me from near-strangulation but also because Andy Nebula, as Meta had pointed out, should be in mirrorcloth, not funereal black. Still, Qualls must think this hydra could boost my career, so I'd better play it to the hilt. "Sorry, octofriend, thought I'd scanned you before," I said, plopping down on the stool next to the hydra. "Whirligig," I said to the bartender, and, "What's powering, manager-man?" to Qualls.

The bartender turned quickly away. I'd once spent an evening teaching him Fistfight City slang. He'd almost died laughing.

Keeping three eyes aimed at me, the hydra focused the fourth on Qualls. "Octofriend?"

"Just a word, gladeye. Insignificant mass. I'm Andy Nebula."

"Yes, Mr. Qualls has provided images," said the hydra. "I am sorry for seizing you so impolitely." He (I remembered what Rain had told me, that every hydra seen in human space was male) had obviously been around humans quite a bit; he held out a tentacle, and I took it momentarily, remembering how I'd almost jumped out of my skin the first time Rain touched me. This time, I didn't even flinch. "My name is—" The hydra made a sound like glass breaking.

I couldn't help wincing. "Tuneful," I said, "but don't you have a label in a lower register?"

"Our guest is usually called The Dealer by his human associates," Qualls said.

"The Dealer?" I laughed. "Better hope the sleazeoids don't get hold of that. They'll be datadumping all over the starnet, saying Andy Nebula's got a private flashpusher."

"Flashpusher?" said The Dealer.

Qualls hastily tapped the screen of his handcomp. "(Moan-scream-whistle-thud)," it said.

"Ah," said The Dealer. "A joke. Ha ha ha." His "laugh" had no inflection at all.

Qualls looked from the alien to me. "The Dealer," he said, "may have a gig for you after this tour is over."

"Orbital!" I said. "Download details!"

"It is tentative," said The Dealer. "However, the venue would be my home world. And it would be a long-term engagement."

"It could help you make the transition from Sensation Single to a, ah, more rounded performer," said Qualls. "If you are interested in continuing your career, that is. Are you?"

Am I! I squelched my initial reaction. Wouldn't do to appear *too* eager. "Could be, manager-man. You think these orange octopeople would still scan me when I'm not Andy Nebula?"

"I think you would be very popular on Hydra," said Qualls. "From your enthusiastic greeting of The Dealer here, I take it you remember the hydra you were with when we first met?"

"Rain? Yeah."

"You'll recall he was quite impressed with you."

"But that was my own music, not this Sensation Single shi...uh, not my current material." Oops, I was forgetting the street slang. But maybe it wasn't important. If the hydras would let me play my own music, it could be the break I'd been hoping for, the chance to stay in music even after Sensation Singles, Inc. dumped me. It wasn't impossible: Pyotr Vasilovich, one of the Pleasure Planets' most famous and enduring stars, had been the very first Single, known as the Parsec Prince, a few years before I was born.

"Precisely," Qualls said. "We'd design a whole new show around *your* music." He shrugged. "And one or two popular cover tunes, of course."

"I wouldn't be working for Sensation Singles anymore?"

"No. I assume you could live with that?"

"Smoothly, gladeye. Intensely smoothly."

"Of course, I would hope to continue as your manager..."

"Activate this and I'm yours 'til termination, gladeye."

Qualls's smile widened, revealing teeth. "Excellent! Once The Dealer and I have come to a final understanding, I'll prepare a contract. I'll send it to your room later."

I took the hint. "I'm lifting," I said. "Orbital tugging your tentacle, Dealer. Down the timestream, manager-man."

"See you, Andy. Now, then, Dealer..." Qualls lowered his voice and bent toward The Dealer. I took my glass of whirligig with me, wondering if I could get a hardcopy of the contract so I could make that driver eat it.

I stopped at the main entrance to the hold and scanned an electronic schematic of the space beyond. Green, green, and more green: we were loaded, sealed, and ready to lift. I palmed the lockplate, and the massive pressure door slid open to admit me.

The forward part of the ship was like any other spacecraft—well, any other ridiculously luxurious spacecraft with artificial gravity and over-the-top ostentatious interior design—but the hold was more like a small village. Modules stood alone in the vast echoing space, connected not by corridors but by lighted pathways. The hold even smelled different: it was still mostly full of planetary air, with all its odours of growing things and people and machines. That smell would linger, despite the constantly recirculating shipboard air, until a new burst of planetary air replaced it at our next port of call.

The forward part of the hold held the various personnel modules. The aft part was reserved for the onboard auditorium, featuring a full-sized stage (where I rehearsed) and seating for maybe two hundred guests for special performances —not that I'd ever performed for anyone there. The metal deck concealed the engine room and gravity-field generators, and the metal ceiling, studded with lights, hid thick shielding and insulation. Once we lifted through the sky of Carstair's Folly, there'd be nothing on the other side of that rather thin shell but vacuum.

Overhead, a blinking green light told anyone interested that the huge cargo doors were space-secured, which I always found reassuring. On the first few legs of the tour I occasionally had nightmares about those doors opening in space, spewing all of us out into the ship's wake. And blinking green light or not, I still made sure the airtight door of my dressing-room module was space-secured whenever I was in it.

Of course, it was shut and sealed now, but out of habit I checked the telltales beside the lockplate as I opened the door— and frowned. The internal life-support system had already activated. It wasn't supposed to do that unless its sensors indicated a living creature needed the oxygen. "Great," I muttered. "Must have picked up a rat."

But inside, the module seemed as empty as it should be. Nothing lurked in the bedroom or the bathroom or the little lounge. I shrugged, called up a Pyotr Vasilovich greatest-hits playlist on the computer, cranked up the volume, kicked off my shoes, propped myself up on my bed, sipped what was left of my whirligig, and finally began to relax, for the first time since I'd come off stage.

After a few minutes I set the empty glass on the side table and closed my eyes, enjoying Pyotr's unique wailing vocals. He was singing something mournful about purple skies and golden eyes...or maybe purple eyes and golden skies...

Crash! I jerked awake. Pyotr's wailing was now underscored by a deep rumble—the engines, warming up. But that wasn't what had woken me. The crash had been closer—in my room!

Security had already failed me twice that evening—what was the name of that Single who had been murdered by a fan...?

I stared around the room, but couldn't see anyone, and no indication of what had made the crash—

Wait a minute. The whirligig glass had vanished. I relaxed, laughing at myself. The ship's vibration had obviously shaken it off the table. I rolled onto my stomach and peered over the edge of the bed—

—into the wide blue eyes of Meta.

6

META MOVES IN

SHE SMILED TENTATIVELY. "Told you I'd see you again!" she said over the rising moan of the engines.

I stared at her. This couldn't be happening. For a moment I didn't say anything, because the first words that came to mind were ones pretty little Meta had probably never heard before. I finally settled on, "What do you think you're *doing*?"

"I've never been in a spaceship before," Meta said, still lying on her back, staring up at me. "I thought it would be fun to see if I could sneak onto yours before you left, and you told me the dressing room was going to be moved on board, so I just slipped back in here after you left it backstage but before they sealed it and I slid under the bed but then I got scared when you came in and decided to try to sneak out before you woke up but I hit the table and the glass broke and—you're not mad, are you?"

I shook my head. You almost had to admire her. Almost. "Look, Meta, do you hear that sound?"

"Yes, and I was wondering—"

"That's the sound of our lift engines. In—oh, I'd say about thirty seconds—we're going to take off. Five minutes after that, we'll be in outer space."

Her face turned white. "What?" She grabbed the edge of the bedframe, scooted out past the broken glass, scrambled up, and ran for the door. "I've got to get out of here—"

She was quick, but I was quicker. I rolled off the bed and grabbed her arm before she could touch the lockplate. "It's too late!" The engines' pitch rose a minor third. "We've lifted."

The moment I touched her, she froze; and then she squealed, a full three octaves higher than the engines—in fact, she sounded a bit like Rain or the Dealer telling me their names. "Andy Nebula touched me!"

I let go of her as though she were red hot. "Will you stop the Andy Nebula biowaste? I told you, when I'm not on stage, I'm not Andy Nebula. I'm just Kit."

She didn't seem to hear me. She was positively vibrating. "I can't believe it! I got into Andy Nebula's dressing room, I talked to him, he touched me, I'm going into space aboard his—ooh, I can't wait to tell Bekka and Roo and—"

"You're going to have to," I said, more harshly than I intended, but I had to get through to her somehow. "You won't be seeing them any time soon."

"What?" That penetrated, all right. "But once you tell the crew I'm on board, won't they—"

"Turn around and land?" I shook my head. "Meta, do you have any idea how much it costs to operate a spaceship?" Actually, I didn't, either, but I knew it was a lot, even by Sensation Single standards. "Landing and taking off are the most expensive." That much I knew. The engines' pitch suddenly slid down a perfect fourth. "Hear that? We're boosting for orbit. There's no way this ship is going back now. You're stuck here until we get to our next stop and Qualls can put you on a commercial flight home."

Meta had gone pale again. "How long?"

"A week."

"A *week*?" She gaped at me, then suddenly lunged at the door again, this time getting it open before I grabbed her. "Let go!" she said, struggling in my grasp. "I have to tell my parents—"

"We will, we will," I said soothingly. "But don't you think it would make more sense for me to take you where you have to go to do that than for you to run aimlessly around the ship?"

She subsided, wiping her eyes, and suddenly laughed a little. "I'm sorry. I'm all right now."

"You're sure?"

"I'm sure." She bent her head back and batted her eyes at me. "But you don't have to let go of me if you don't want to..."

I let go of her so fast she half-fell against the bulkhead. "Let's take you to face the music."

Meta gazed as wide-eyed at everything we passed on our way to the bridge as I had the first time *I* came on board. *The Bullet* impressed everyone (which was the idea, of course). I doubted you'd find many other ships with corridors panelled in real Earth oak, floored with deep golden carpets, and lit by crystal fixtures. Here and there, tiny holovids of previous Singles endlessly repeated the dance steps that had made them—briefly—famous. If you stopped by one, the sound came up, too. I never stopped, because the last thing I wanted to hear was *more* Sensation Singles, but Meta would have listened to every one of them if I hadn't insisted she keep moving. "I don't know how far it is to jump-off," I pointed out, "and we can't send a message once we're in alternity. You don't want your parents thinking you've vanished into thin air, and *we* don't want to be charged with kidnapping. You'll have plenty of time to explore the ship after this is all settled."

"Right," Meta said, but she still moved reluctantly away from a holo of Phil FreeLight singing *Program Your Love,* the syrupiest Single of them all, which was saying something. *Are all teenaged girls on the Pleasure Planets this spaceheaded?* I wondered. Public image to the contrary, I was not an expert on girls from *any* planet. The "girls" I'd known in Fistfight City were hard as duracrete and meaner than spaceport rats, while as Andy Nebula, the only girls I saw were the screaming ones in the audience. Only carefully planned and managed scandals were permitted Sensation Singles, and so Meta was the first girl I'd been close enough to touch during my entire tour.

A sudden shift in decor from flamboyant to utilitarian marked our arrival in Ship's Operations. I'd sometimes wondered what *The Bullet*'s crew thought of all the Singles they'd seen come and go, but after my earlier conversation with the chauffeur, I thought maybe I was better off not knowing.

Second Mate Fister, whom we found in a wardroom near the bridge, was *not* pleased. A small, stout woman with a speaking voice half an octave lower than mine, she frowned ferociously at Meta. "What the *blazes* did you think you were playing at?" she boomed, and Meta shrank back against me. "Do you know what interstellar law gives us the right to do to stowaways? *Do you?*"

Meta shook her head.

"It says we can space you. Did you think of that before you—"

I knew the Second Mate only wanted to scare Meta, to make her see how stupid she'd been. I'd tried to do the same thing. But suddenly, I didn't like it very much. After all, Meta was *my* fan. "End program," I snapped at her. "We don't have time for this. You know, and I know, you're not going to space her, but you're going to worry her parents sick and get us in legal trouble if we don't get a message to them before jump-off. So, are you going to let us use ship communications or not?"

The Second Mate flushed, and her jaw clenched—but I was still the current Single and therefore carried considerable weight on board *The Bullet,* even though I'd never thrown it around before. Seeing the fire in the Second Mate's eyes, I decided I wouldn't try to throw it around again. But just this once—

"Ten minutes to jump-off," she growled at me. "You and your 'friend'—" she managed to make the word sound insulting, and I flushed even though I had nothing to be ashamed of —"can use communications."

"Thank you." I pulled Meta out of there before the Second Mate could change her mind.

Bob Hosking, the crewman on duty in the communications room, grinned at me as I came in. "Hi, Andy." He nodded at Meta. "Who's your lady friend?"

"Hi, Bob. Stowaway, believe it or not. Fister says you're to let her use communications to call her parents."

"Sure." Hosking smiled at Meta and poised his fingers over the controls. "Access code?"

Meta reeled out a string of letters and numbers that Hosking echoed into the console. After a moment's lightspeed delay, a screen lit with a written message, repeated by a woman's voice. "This is the Prescott home artificial intelligence. At the moment no human is available to speak to you. Do you wish to leave a message?"

Meta sat down in front of the console. "Milly, this is Meta."

"Identity confirmed. Hello, Meta."

"Are my parents really not at home or are you just in intercept mode?"

"Your parents are attending a reception at the Administrator's Residence," the computer said.

Meta said a word that surprised me.

Milly replied primly, "My programming requires me to warn you, Meta, that the word just uttered is not considered acceptable vocabulary by your parents."

"Sorry. Look, take a message for me, will you—"

"Thirty seconds to jump-off," a different computer said.

"You'll have to hurry," Hosking warned Meta.

"Recording," said Milly.

"Mom, Dad, I'm all right, but I won't be home for about a week," Meta said rapidly. "I met Andy Nebula and he's really nice. He asked me to come with him to his next concert, and I was so excited I said yes. But I'll come back right afterward. Be sure to tell Bekka and Roo! 'Bye!"

"Wait a minute—" I began, but "Jump-off in ten...nine...eight..." said the ship, and "Contact broken," said Hosking, and then came the twisting-bent-sideways-turned-inside-out disorientation of the translation into alternity, and then it was too late to do anything about what Meta had just told her parents.

"Wow!" said Meta. "What a ride!"

I groaned and massaged the back of my neck. "Yeah," I muttered. "What a ride."

"Mr. Nebula," said Second Mate Fister's voice over the ship's intercom, her tone dangerously sweet. "Please report to the passenger lounge."

7

A CHANGE OF PLANS

Qualls met us in the lounge. "Wonderful," he said, surveying Meta as she stared eagerly around. "Just wonderful. We'll be lucky if the police aren't waiting for us next planetfall."

That brought Meta's head around. "Oh, no," she said. "I sent a message to my parents."

"I reviewed your 'message.' Why didn't you tell the truth?"

Meta looked abashed—but only a little. "I'm sorry. I guess I wanted to impress them—and my friends."

"Well, you're going to have to send another message when we slip back into realspace. I'm afraid you're going to be gone longer than a week."

"What?" said Meta.

"Why?" I echoed.

"There's been a change of plans."

"A change of plans?" I felt a chill. "Ticket sales—?"

"Next to nothing. We've cancelled all the remaining tour dates except the final one, and we're moving it forward."

"But you said Mr. Karpov had agreed to at least four more—"

"This change is my idea."

"Your idea?" I felt my face flush. "You cancelled three of my performances without even asking me?"

"I did ask you."

"When?"

"Just a couple of hours ago, right here. You agreed to a long-term engagement on Hydra, remember?"

"What's that got to do with—"

"That engagement starts before the tour would have been over. I tried to talk The Dealer into pushing the opening back, but he was adamant. I assumed you would consider holding onto this post-tour deal more important than playing a couple of dates before half-empty houses, but if you'd like, I can probably still cancel—"

"*No!*" I almost shouted. Then I took a deep breath. "No, of course not," I said, more calmly. I tried on a grin; it fit pretty well. "All's optimal, gladeye."

Qualls grimaced.

Meta had been following this conversation like a spectator at a tri-ball match. "But what about me?"

"What about you?" Qualls snapped, and this time I didn't feel much like standing up for her. She'd been nothing but trouble from the minute she'd sneaked into my dressing room, and she'd as much as told her parents I'd seduced her. I wondered if I could sue her for defamation of character. *Oh, well —maybe a good mudsplatter from the sleazeoids will boost the crowd at my last show.*

"You can send another message between jump-offs," Qualls

told Meta, "but we're not landing, and you won't be able to get a ship until we reach the closing venue of the tour."

"Where's that?"

"Kit's hometown."

I stared at Qualls. "Fistfight City? You never said—"

"You never asked."

Some excuse, but I let it go. So, I was going to return to Fistfight City as the hometown-boy-made good. I hoped I'd draw a crowd. I hoped the Ice Boys came—however many of them flash had left alive. However many still had brain enough to remember me.

Any worry Meta felt about the extra time away from home vanished in sudden excitement. "But that's great!" she said, turning to me with wide eyes. "You can show me all those places in your bio—the store where the owner gave you your beat-up old stringsynth because he could tell you really loved music, the park where you sang your first song and the kind old lady gave you—"

"Yeah, right," I said. As I've mentioned, my official bio was worth considerably less than the chip it was stored on. I guess you could say that a store owner had "given" me the stringsynth, since I certainly hadn't paid for it, but he hadn't been aware of his generosity, being home in bed when I broke his shop's front window. "I doubt you're going to be there long enough."

"Take her to any of the empty guest quarters," Qualls said.

I started to ask why a crewman couldn't do that, but Qualls had turned his back on us. Irritated, I led Meta out.

More holovids of former Singles lined the corridor running to the guest quarters. Meta listed them happily as we passed.

"That's Flashpoint Charlie, and there's The Toneman, and that's Rubberneck, and—oh, look, that's Paris Paradise!"

I stopped dead. "Paris Paradise? Are you sure?"

"Of course, I'm sure," Meta said, in a don't-be-silly tone. "I know all the Singles."

I hurried back to the holo. "What's wrong?" Meta asked.

The sound came up as I stopped by the alcove.

A planet can be a paradise,
A comet can be a paradise,
A twirling asteroid can be a paradise for two,
If the two are you and me together,
Here today and there forever...

Grimacing at the sappy tune and bad rhyming, I leaned closer, trying to get a clear look at the little twirling figure's face, but the resolution wasn't good enough.

Anyway, it couldn't be. The old flashman had been in his fifties. Paris Paradise the Sensation Single couldn't be more than twenty-one by now, because all Singles were teenagers. Just because he had claimed to be Paris Paradise...anybody could claim to be anybody. Before he met me, he probably told half a dozen other people he was Andy Nebula.

But still, that name, and that warning about someone or something getting him, getting her, getting me, too...I didn't like it. If something like that had happened on the street, I would have lifted, fast. That's the way you find out about threats on the street—garbled whispers and half-heard rumours. It doesn't pay to wait for proof that a flashgang is taking over the burned-out building where you've been flopping, or that the meatmen are stocking up, or the 'forcers are planning a sweep. If the street is tense, you lift—if you can. I'd always been able to, because I fed myself with my stringsynth. But this time, I couldn't.

On the other hand, this wasn't the street.

"Have you met him?" asked Meta.

"No. I mean, I thought maybe I did—but I guess I was wrong." I straightened and strode firmly on down the corridor. "Let's get you settled so *I* can get some sleep."

Meta's new quarters weren't much farther. I showed her how to slave the lockpad to her handprint, and she opened the door and stepped inside. The lights came up, revealing a smaller version of my own dressing room—sleeping area, sitting room, bathroom. No kitchen like mine had, but on the other hand, the furnishings were far more ornate—dark wood and plush red carpet and paintings on the walls. Meta bounced on the bed, then grinned at me. "This is great! I'm *glad* I won't be able to go home for a month. This has all worked out so much better than I expected. It really is just like your song, you know?"

"It's not *my* song," I snapped. "It was written for me by a computer. You've never heard *my* music, unless you used to hang out on street corners in Fistfight City."

"Then why don't you play some for me?"

"No. It's late, I'm tired, and I've got a lot to think about. Good night."

"Tomorrow?" Meta called after me as I went out the door.

I didn't reply.

On the way back to my dressing room I studied the holovids I passed. Who had all these kids been, really? Had any of *them* dreamed of being more than a Sensation Single? Had any of them made it? Sure, there was Pyotr, but he'd been the very first Single, more than twenty years ago. Since then at least forty had come and gone—maybe more, since some only lasted a couple of months. But aside from Pyotr and the one murdered by a fan—StarMaid, that was her name, I remembered now—I knew nothing about any of them.

Time to find out, then. I resolved to do some extensive digging in the computer.

Tomorrow. Right now, all I was looking for was sleep.

Fifteen minutes later, in my dressing room (and after a quick check under the bed—well, you never know), I found it.

8

STREETSENSE WARNING

As USUAL, in the morning, all the vague fears of the night before seemed foolish. Oh, I still intended to research the fates of my predecessors, but it didn't seem nearly as urgent. Besides, we were two weeks from Fistfight City. Plenty of time.

I ate breakfast alone in my room, but I was only halfway through my poached smokebird when Meta knocked. (Somehow, I knew it was her even before I checked the security monitor.) *At least she knocked this time,* I thought, cinching up the fuzzy bathrobe I'd put on when I'd come out of the shower.

Somewhat reluctantly, I let her in. She bustled in with a level of energy I found disgusting at that time of shipday. "Good morning!" she chirped. "Why, you're not even dressed yet, sleepyhead."

"I wasn't expecting visitors," I said, and went back to my breakfast tray.

"Mmmm, that looks good. Better than what I had." She plopped down on the bed. "So, what are we going to do today?"

"We?" I picked up my coffee cup, drank the last swallow, and put the cup back on the tray. "Look, Meta, in case you've forgotten, I'm a professional entertainer. I've got work to do. I can't be—"

"You mean you'll be rehearsing, and stuff like that?"

Actually, I seldom rehearsed anymore, but if it would keep her off my back... "Yeah, stuff like that."

"I'll watch!"

"You can't. It's—a closed rehearsal." I shrugged. "I don't make the rules." Although I'd just made up *that* one. "Can't have the public seeing Andy Nebula flubbing a dance step."

"Can't have the public seeing Andy Nebula in his bathrobe, either," Meta pointed out, "or only wearing...well, not exactly *wearing*...a towel, but..."

Another knock rescued me from having to respond to *that*. "What is this, Earth Central Spaceport?" I growled. I stomped (or tried to—barefoot stomping doesn't actually work very well) over to the door and opened it to discover some Sensation Single Inc. employee or other (they always seemed interchangeable to me, like glowtubes) standing there.

The young man's eyes slipped to Meta, sitting on the bed, then back to me, barefoot in my bathrobe. I groaned inwardly. "Sorry to interrupt, Andy, but Mr. Qualls and Mr. Marcel need to see you in the passenger lounge as soon as is convenient."

"I'll be there in ten minutes." I shut the door in his face and turned back to Meta. "You heard. I have to get dressed."

She stayed put and gave me an expectant look. "Don't let me stop you."

"Get out!"

She laughed and stood up. "Later, then, gladeye. You can give me the grand tour!" She swept out.

"Not if I can avoid it," I said to the closed door.

Much to my astonishment, I discovered I really *did* have to rehearse. In fact, for the rest of the journey Qualls and Marcel worked me harder than they had since my initial few weeks. I didn't even have to find excuses not to see Meta—not that she seemed to miss me: as far as I could tell, everyone on board loved her, even the Second Mate, whom I surprised giving her a tour of the hold as I came off the stage, dripping with sweat, one afternoon. Meta waved gaily to me; the Second Mate gave me a look as cold as a cryosleep pod, as though daring me comment. I didn't.

"But why do I have to rehearse so much?" I complained to Marcel a day or two later. "I could sing and dance this deadhead Single in my sleep!"

"Take it up with Qualls," Marcel grunted, heaving a misplaced fogmaker back into position. "I just run the stage."

I stomped off, determined to do exactly that. This was crazy! I only had to perform this drivel once more, then I'd be performing my own music on Hydra. *That* was what I should be rehearsing.

I found Qualls in the lounge with—*biowaste!* Nobody had told me The Dealer was still aboard. Time to haul out my "home babble" again. "Hey, gladeyes!" I called. "Mr. Dealer, old octofriend. Thought you lifted back on Carstair's Folly."

All four of The Dealer's eyes twisted around to stare at me. "I have business in Fistfight City," his androgynous voice said. "Mr. Qualls was good enough to offer me passage."

"We're rather busy—" Qualls said irritably, but I had plenty of irritation of my own; I slid onto a stool beside The Dealer.

"Well, I'd say it's high-prob that business between you and octodude here has something to do with me," I said cheerfully to Qualls, and gave him a bright, toothy smile.

He scowled back.

"We are indeed discussing your future," said The Dealer. "I have been outlining for Mr. Qualls the details of your scheduled stay on my home world."

"Orbital! My file on that's definitely data-poor. What's the high-accuracy bytestuff, Mr. Manager?"

"It's not entirely settled," Qualls said. "There are still a few points to finalize."

"I'm linked!"

"Excuse us just a moment," Qualls said to The Dealer. Then he grabbed my arm and dragged me into the farthest corner of the lounge. "What are you trying to do?" he whisper-growled. "You don't know how to deal with the hydras. If you keep sticking your face into negotiations the whole thing could fall apart."

"Then how about filling me in on what you've already decided?" I growled back. "Or is it too much to ask that I be told something about my own future?"

Qualls shot a glance at The Dealer, who was literally keeping one eye cocked at us. "All right, all right. But not now. Later. For now, get out of here."

"Not just yet," I said. "I really came to find out why you've got me rehearsing night and day. I've only got to sing 'From the Street to the Stars' once more, and you *know* I know it perfectly."

"It's got to be better than perfect in Fistfight City if you want to sign on with The Dealer."

"But if I'm going to be doing my own music on Hydra—"

"It's three weeks to Hydra. Plenty of time to rehearse then."

"Is there a problem, Mr. Qualls?" called The Dealer.

"No!" Qualls said. As he turned his head, I saw sweat glistening on his forehead. "Just a technical matter." He swung his eyes back to me. "Look, I told you, let Marcel handle it," he said loudly, then pushed me toward the door.

This time I took the none-too-subtle hint, but I stopped just outside, looking back as the door slid closed behind me. The Dealer had Qualls scared spitless. But why? My future was on the line, not his. For him, this should just be an ordinary business deal, but clearly, it wasn't.

Maybe he's got a gambling debt, I thought. Then another thought struck me. *Or maybe he's been embezzling money from the company.*

That made some kind of sense, and would certainly explain why he was so nervous. *I should probably feel flattered he thinks he can make money off me.*

Huh. I didn't feel very flattered.

I walked slowly back toward the hold, pausing again by the holo of Paris Paradise (not *too* near, since I didn't want to activate his annoying song). I wondered if anybody would stop and listen to "From the Street to the Stars" when *I* was just a holo in a little alcove like that. "Were things this crazy when you were a Single?" I asked Paris. He just kept dancing.

I'd put it off long enough; it was time I followed up on my vow to find out what had happened to Paris—to all of them. If I could just get some time off from rehearsing...

I finally got my chance, two days from Fistfight City, thanks to an equipment malfunction. One of the holoprojectors blew a something-or-other, causing half of the flashgang I supposedly held harmless through the brilliance of my dancing to suddenly freeze in place. Holos or not, I still winced as, unable to stop, I whirled through eight of them. (I was just lucky it wasn't the robodancer troupe. Those things weigh a tonne.)

The synths switched off abruptly and Marcel's creative curses echoed from the control booth. "Done for the day, Kit," he finally said, once he'd run out of obscenities (I resolved to ask him what some of the words meant later). "Richter, where the sucking vacuum did you put the..." his voice faded away.

I lifted before he could change his mind, and a few minutes later finally sat down at my computer terminal, where the first thing I discovered was a message from Meta. I quieted a pang of guilt at having ignored her. If she could charm the Second Mate she could obviously take care of herself.

"Hi, Andy," her recorded image said.

"Kit!" I snapped. The recording ignored me, of course, but then, the real girl probably would have, too.

"Can't seem to get more than a second or two with you, so I thought I'd leave this to let you know I messaged my parents at the last jump-off. Of course, they won't get it until the courier capsule makes it out of alternity at Carstair's Folly, but anyway, I told them I was fine and that there'd been a change of plans and I'd be back even later than I thought, but not to worry because I was with you and having a wonderful time. I just wish I could see Bekka's face...anyway, if you ever have some time when you're not rehearsing, I hope we can do something together. All right? 'Bye. And I don't care if your tour is winding down, I still think Andy Nebula is the best Sensation Single ever!" Her picture went away, but it left me feeling guilty again. Here I *did* have some time off rehearsing, and I was planning to spend it with my computer.

Oh, come on, I told myself then. *So what? You don't owe her anything. She pushed herself on you. Besides, she'd rather make up stories about all the fun she's had with Andy Nebula than face the dull reality.*

I put Meta out of my mind, cleared the screen, and asked for current information on former Singles.

I drew the computer equivalent of a blank stare. There *was* no current information on any former Sensation Singles, except for old Pyotr and poor dead StarMaid. All the rest had dropped out of sight. For some, nothing at all existed except the official Sensation Single bio—and I knew how trustworthy *that* was. I did find out a few real names—Rubberneck was a kid called Kim Ng, for example, from an extremely out-of-the-way planet with the improbable name of Piggyback—but even that didn't help much. Kim Ng had had very little history before he became Rubberneck and none at all afterward. He just disappeared.

I dug even harder for something on Paris Paradise, with little more success. His real name was Adrien Chapdelaine, and he'd been born in the ancient city of Paris on old Earth itself—hence his stage name. No records of a family, no home address, nothing but an Earth World Authority census number. And after his brief reign as a Single—nothing at all.

"Nobody just vanishes," I muttered. I called up my own file —and was chilled by the similarity to Adrien Chapdelaine's. No family, no home address, not even a government number, since the Murdochian government couldn't care less whether I existed and had apparently never linked me to the kid who'd run away from a Fistfight City orphanage years before. I'd probably never even been reported missing. Heck, knowing *that* place, it was probably still collecting government feds for my room and board.

What worried me more was that, apart from Pyotr, none of them seemed to have had any kind of musical career, post-Single. I was heading to Hydra. Surely a concert tour like that would make the media. I couldn't believe not *one* of those dozens of former Singles had ever tried to continue his or her career like I was, or that all of them had failed so completely as to leave no trace.

I tried to tell myself I was being crazy, worrying about nothing, but streetsense, based on seven years of living off my wits, overpowered Andy Nebula's version of common sense, based on a few months of having things given to him on a platter. Before I sang a note in Fistfight City, I'd know the truth—and I thought I knew who could tell it to me.

"Not as old as you might think," Marcel had said about the flashman who called himself Paris Paradise, and, "No, I didn't know him—I just meant flash ages a man."

I headed back to the stage.

9

HOMECOMING

Finding Marcel was easy: he was on the rehearsal stage. Getting him to talk wasn't. I strode up to him with all the impetus of my suspicions. "Look, Marcel, I need to—"

"No, no, no!" he yelled, not at me but at the unfortunate Richter, who had wandered into his line of sight. "Not there! You expect lasers to go around corners, now? Check your marks next time!" He shot me an irritable glance. "What do *you* want?"

"I need to talk to you, Marcel, about—"

Something beeped. "I'm a little busy right now, Kit. We're not going to be able to fix that blown holo projector before the show, so I've got to rearrange the ones we have to cover the gap —yes, what is it?" he said into a hand communicator.

I waited while he irritably explained to somebody on the other end that if two stagebots were trying to install each other as lighting units then one or both of them obviously had a serious programming deficiency and the only way to stop them was to turn them both off. "Then pull their chips and run a diagnostic. Isn't that obvious? Did you really have to ask?" He stuck the communicator back in his pocket. "I don't know where the company finds these idiots..." he muttered.

I took my chance. "Marcel, I need to talk to you about Paris Paradise."

Did he twitch at the name, just a little? "What about him?" He jumped down from the stage and headed up the aisle toward the control booth. I followed him.

"Did you know him?"

"Of course I knew him. I've been stage manager for every Single for the last ten years."

"Do you know what happened to him?"

"Went back to Paris, I suppose. What do you care?" He reached the control booth and palmed the lockplate.

"That flashman who got backstage on Carstair's Folly—"

The door opened, and Marcel went in. "Yeah?"

"He said he was Paris Paradise."

"So? Look, Andy, I've got a lot of—"

"Was he?"

Marcel flipped switches without looking at me. "Paris was just a kid like you when I knew him a couple of years ago. That flashman was a lot older than I am. How could it have been Paris?"

"You tell me."

"Ten minutes to test," Marcel said into a microphone, his voice booming on the stage. Then he turned to face me. "I know you're nervous about the end of your run, Kit—"

"That's not—"

"—but we've got some big problems with the equipment

right now and I just don't have time for this nonsense. I don't keep tabs on ex-Singles. Once they're out of my sight, they're no concern of mine. And out of my sight is where I want you right now, you understand?" He pointed toward my dressing room. "Now!"

I glared at him, then stalked off into the darkness of the hold. He knew something, I was sure of it. But what could he be hiding? That that flashman really *had* been Paris Paradise? That was just crazy...

I groaned as I got closer to my dressing room and saw Meta sitting outside it with her back to the door. She scrambled up and waved as I came closer. "Andy!"

"Kit," I said.

"Sorry, Kit...I heard you had to quit rehearsing, so I thought —did you know there's a pool on this ship? We could go swimming—"

"No, we couldn't. Listen, Meta, you're a great kid, and I'm really happy you're a fan of Sensation Singles, but I'm only going to be a Single for a few more days and after that I've got a whole new career to worry about, and that means that right now I've got a lot of thinking to do. So why don't you just go off and pester someone else and leave me alone?"

Her smile faded, and her face turned white; then, without a word, she turned and ran out of the hold. I took half a step after her, then stopped, shrugged, and went into the dressing room. She'd be going home as soon as we got to Fistfight City anyway, and I really didn't need her added to my list of things to worry about. Besides, if there was something nasty going on behind the scenes, I'd be doing her a favour by keeping her out of it.

MY RESPITE from rehearsal didn't last. After supper and late into the night Marcel had me back at it, with no let-up for the rest of the trip. I didn't complain, this time; the altered holoprojector array changed several of the dance sequences drastically, and I had to work hard to polish them to performance level. Qualls wasn't happy about it, either. I heard him yelling backstage when I entered the rehearsal theatre the day before we were scheduled to land in Fistfight City. "...concert is crucial! If this contract with The Dealer falls through, you'll never work again!"

I couldn't hear Marcel's reply, but Qualls's voice suddenly boomed even louder. "Don't try to shift the blame. The company's been cutting expenses. If you couldn't do the job with the budget you were given you should have said so, and we would have found someone who could."

Sensation Singles cutting expenses? First I'd heard of it. *Very* interesting. I decided not to announce my arrival just yet. I headed down the aisle to the front row, where I could hear them as clearly as if they were performing for my benefit.

"Maybe you should be doing some cutting back of your own," Marcel snapped. "Then you wouldn't need your little sideline. It seems to be putting you under a great deal of strain."

Qualls quit shouting. Instead, his voice turned low and poisonous. "My 'little sideline' is none of your business. You don't talk about it—not even to me. You *know* why."

Silence. Then, "Yeah, I know."

"Good. Then you also know that it is in your best interest to ensure that my 'sideline' remains profitable. So, get back to work, Stage Manager. I'm sure the little streetslug will be arriving for rehearsal very shortly, and I don't want to see him."

If he'd come onstage then I would have been caught, but instead, I heard him slam out through the backstage right exit… and then heard Marcel say, in a low voice, "I don't blame you."

I resisted the urge to chase Qualls and strangle him with my bare hands. *Streetslug?* And I was putting my future in *his* hands?

And what "sideline?" *Yeah, I'm a streetslug, all right,* I thought. *I know slime when I step in it.*

But just what was that slime made of? I wanted to pressure Marcel for an answer, but it sounded like Qualls was standing over him with a pretty big stick. *Too dangerous,* I decided—at least, too dangerous on the ship. Once we were down in Fistfight City, *my* orbit, if I didn't like the scan, I could lift…

Oh, yeah? I told myself sarcastically. *And then what?*

If I lifted before the show, I breached my contract, and Andy Nebula's credit stayed behind. Then what? Back to living hand-to-mouth as a street musician? Scrounging food, hiding and running from flashgangs and meatmen, until one day I didn't hide well enough or run fast enough?

Maybe I'm overprogramming here. Maybe Qualls's little scheme is just a scam—negotiate a bigger deal with The Dealer than he'll tell me about and keep most of it for himself. I might even let him get away with it. The important thing about the Hydran gig is that I'll be playing my music my way.

Holding that thought firmly in mind, I cleared my throat, then marched cheerfully and noisily onto the stage to begin rehearsing.

The next day we made planetfall, timing our landing to roughly synchronize shiptime with local Fistfight City time. I stood on the duracrete, watching the cranes lift the modules from the hold, my dressing room among them, breathing chilly air full of the sharp tang of rocket exhaust and ozone, looking up at the cold, austere mountains beyond the city...and wishing I was somewhere else. *Anywhere* else.

So much for the old hometown. Give me the Pleasure Planets any day.

But there I was, and I had a concert to give. I looked at the spaceport's main terminal and grinned a little. This time I'd walk through there with nothing to fear except hordes of fans and media.

Did I say hordes? An hour later Qualls and I and a half-dozen Sensation Single staff made our grand entrance through customs, and while a group of people formed to ogle and photograph, it was far from a horde, or even a throng. More like an intimate gathering, at least compared to the crowds that had greeted me everywhere in the early days of the Single.

Meta had joined us when we boarded the ground transport from ship to terminal, looking subdued and not meeting my eyes. *Well, she'll be gone soon, anyway,* I told myself. *Probably even before the concert.* As if to confirm it, Qualls whisked her off somewhere before we were out of the terminal, presumably to arrange for her return to Carstair's Folly.

That's that, I thought. *I'll never see her again.* I wondered what exotic lies she would tell her friends about me.

I couldn't help looking closely at every mirrored pillar in the terminal, but Dry Ice, if he still lived, didn't put in an appearance, even to mock. Once, I thought I caught a glimpse of Hydran orange in the distance, and imagined it was Rain, soaking up new experiences, but then the crowd shifted, and when I looked again, the flash of colour had vanished.

Shortly thereafter, so did the crowd. By the time we stood on the sidewalk, we could have been any anonymous band of tourists wondering why they'd ever wanted to come to Murdoch IV in the first place (I was willing to bet every band of tourists reached that point sooner or later—usually, sooner). "Are you sure anyone is coming tonight?" I said to Marcel over the rush of cold wind whipping grit into our faces.

"Not my concern," he said, stone-faced and squinty-eyed. "I just set up the stage."

"Thanks for the power-boost, gladeye," I muttered. I looked around for Qualls, but he hadn't come back yet. Instead, I saw the transport coming to take us to the crashball stadium in the north end of town where our stage equipment and dressing rooms had already been hauled.

A sullen drizzle began as we climbed into the transport. I decided to try Marcel again. "I hope their concert tent doesn't leak," I said as I settled by a window in the seat behind him.

He grunted without looking around. "No tent. The stage will be covered but your fans are on their own."

"I should have guessed." I leaned my forehead against the cool glass and watched as familiar rain-slicked streets slid by, even greyer and grimier than I remembered. *You can't have me back,* I told them silently. I didn't much care for my Single, "From the Street to the Stars," but I intended to live up to the title all the same. *I'm sticking to my contract no matter what Qualls is up to. As long as he gets me off this planet again, I don't care if he robs me blind.*

Qualls, without Meta, met us at the stadium, wearing the

same long black weathercoat I'd first seen him in. "Looks like we'll fill ground-level and most of the lower seats," he told me as we crossed the pavement to the shelter of the grandstands. "The rest depends on walk-ups."

"In *this* weather?" The rain pounded the pavement around us, and the spray on the wind had such a wintry bite it wouldn't have surprised me to see it turn to sleet. Qualls, though, didn't seem to notice the cold. I resolved to buy a weathercoat of my own at the first opportunity. "*I* wouldn't come out to hear me on a night like this."

Qualls shrugged. "The Dealer will be here. He's the only one that matters. Look, I've got to make a call. I'll talk to you later." He hurried off, leaving me to find my own way through the grey duracrete tunnels beneath the stands to the fenced, private parking lot where they'd set up my dressing room and the other modules. A runner met me at my door. "Sound and vid check in forty-five minutes, Andy," he said breathlessly.

"Thank you," I told him, and watched him dash away, up the ramp toward the field, feeling odd to know it would be the last time I would hear those words. I turned and palmed my dressing-room lockplate, figuring the feeling would go away as I plunged into the routine of getting ready for a concert.

Instead, it got worse. Each familiar step of preparation was for the last time. Sure, I hoped to perform again—on Hydra and elsewhere—but not as Andy Nebula. I even caught myself thinking that maybe my Single wasn't all that bad a song, all things considered, and trying to remember the faces of the holodancers and 'bots. "Back in my old orbit—data retrieval overload," I muttered.

At last the people came—about 30,000, I guessed, knowing

the capacity of the stadium. Not great, certainly not a sellout, but not too bad, either, considering the weather, the venue...and the planet. The warm-up group, a local glamcrash band called the Glitterbloods, played to half-hearted cheers—then came the knock on my door, "Five minutes," from the runner, and the long walk up the ramp and through the backstage maze. Finally, I stood in the wings in my mirrorcloth tights, listening to the roar of the crowd and the pounding of the synths, watching the lasers building the holos in the smoke and the 'bots glistening in the shadows, and for the first time I realized I didn't want to stop being a Single, that if I could, I'd do it forever.

But I couldn't. I'd reached the end I'd always known would come.

"Break a leg, Kit," Marcel's voice said in my earpiece.

"Thanks, Marcel," I said; and then the opening chords crashed and, for the last time, Andy Nebula danced into the spotlight.

10

TIME TO LIFT

THE RAIN HAD SUBSIDED to a fine mist, leaving the air cool and fresh, and I felt wonderful as I sang and danced and fought my insubstantial enemies and rescued my robotic girl. I couldn't see the crowd, but I could hear them, could sense that I had them, that they were caught up in the story told by the song and the dance, that I held the emotions of all 30,000 of them in the palm of my hand like a lump of clay. They followed every nuance, responded to every subtlety, and rewarded me at the song's end with a standing ovation and the roar of "An-dy! An-dy! An-dy!" over and over.

I came off the stage drenched with sweat and riding a high like I'd never felt, even after my very first concert. To my surprise, Qualls greeted me in person. "Great show, Kit!" he shouted in my ear above the ongoing roar of the crowd. "The Dealer was impressed!"

I gave him a thumbs-up and a grin. Who cared what silly scam involving my money he was up to? It couldn't dampen this moment for me. He clapped me on the shoulder as I went past him, toward the tunnels leading back to the parking lot and my dressing room. "I'll be by later and we'll finalize things," he yelled.

I nodded and kept moving, grabbing the towel I always kept handy backstage and wiping my face as I went. *He'd better come by quick,* I thought. I had no intention of hanging around my dressing room for long. We wouldn't be lifting until the next day, and I planned to celebrate my success by hitting some of the Fistfight City funspots I'd only seen from the outside when I'd lived there. I used to play my stringsynth for the crowds waiting to get in, until the bouncers chased me off. I grinned to myself, picturing those same bouncers fawning all over me now that I was Andy Nebula. Oh, yes, it was going to be a big-time homecoming party night for this boy.

I passed security guards at the various places where access could be gained to the backstage area, and nodded approvingly to each of them in turn. *No more flashmen cornering me in the corridors, and no more surprise visitors to the dressing room,* I thought—and then stumbled to a halt just a few metres from my door, because there *was* someone there, just visible in the shadows. I turned to call for security, but the shadowy figure said, "No, Kit —wait," and stepped into the light.

I stared. "Marcel? What are—why aren't you in the control booth?"

"I left the computer in charge."

"But you're not supposed to do that. What if something went—"

"It didn't, did it? I've got to talk to you without Qualls

knowing, and as long as he thinks I'm up there, he won't suspect that I'm back here."

"Well—" I touched the lockplate and the door slid open. "Come inside, then." Marcel followed me in quickly, taking off the floppy hat he'd worn that had shadowed his face. Like Qualls, he wore a weathercoat.

They give the employees weathercoats but not the star? I thought, a little peeved, tossing my towel on the bed. "Wasn't that a great show?" I said as I headed to the kitchen for a cold drink. My computer terminal blinked at me as I passed. *Fan mail waiting,* I thought smugly. "All that rehearsal really paid off. Qualls sure knew what he was talking about."

"Yeah, Qualls always knows what he's talking about. But I don't think you do."

I turned with an unopened chillpac of icefizz in my hand. "What?"

"I came to tell you—" Marcel took a deep breath. "I came to tell you you've got to dump Qualls as your manager. Now, while you still can."

"Dump him?" I opened the pac and took a swig of cold, tingling sweetness. "He's already got a post-Single gig lined up."

"Believe me, you don't want it."

"Believe me, I *do* want it." I flopped into one of the armchairs by the coffee table. "Andy Nebula's dead and gone, as of tonight. Now there's just me—Kit—and *my* music. And besides, we have a verbal agreement—witnessed by Qualls, The Dealer, and *The Bullet*'s barman. That's binding enough that if I back out now Qualls will tie up all my credit so fast I'll be back singing outside Fistfight City bars."

"You'd be better off."

I gulped more icefizz, then wiped my mouth and pointed the pac at Marcel. "Look, you're not telling me anything I don't know. I know Qualls is up to something—I heard him yelling at you two days ago. I figure he's planning to skim off a big chunk of the money I earn from this Hydra gig." I shrugged. "So what? I've got enough credit from being Andy Nebula to last me all my life—unless I crash Qualls's program. What do I care if he gets rich, too? The important thing is to do the show—to do *my* music."

"No, the important thing is to *not* do the show." Marcel sat down in the chair across the coffee table from me, eyes narrowed and intense. "Listen to me, Kit. You asked about the other Singles. Qualls offered most of them post-Single gigs, too. And where are they now?"

"You tell me."

"I wish I could." Marcel got up again abruptly and paced. "I shouldn't even be telling you this much. If Qualls finds out—"

"What's he got on you?"

Marcel stopped dead, and slowly turned to face me. "That's one thing I *won't* tell you. Just don't ignore this warning, Kit. Tell Qualls you want no part of this Hydra deal, cut your losses and run. You can find another manager, a good one—you've got the talent. You could be another Pyotr—"

"Why are you warning me at all? Why take the risk?" I studied him suspiciously. "What's in it for you?"

"Let's just say it makes it a little bit easier for me to live with myself—a very little."

I frowned. I didn't want this, not tonight, not after that great show. I wanted to keep the high, keep the adrenalin flowing, go out and party, plan my brand-new non-Single show in my head—I didn't want these veiled warnings and dark remarks and, most of all, I didn't want anything to interfere with the bright new future I already had mapped out for myself.

"Fine, you've warned me. Now go away and live with yourself. I'm going to take a shower and change, and then I'm headed out on the town." I emptied the icefizz pac, went back into the kitchen, tossed it into the disposal bin under the sink. "And you'd better get back to the control booth, because Qualls said he'd be coming by here shortly to fill me in on the details of the Hydra deal."

"Kit—"

Suddenly angry, I spun on him. "What? If Qualls is so dangerous, tell me the whole story! Clear your conscience altogether! *Make* me listen to your warning! Otherwise, lift, because I really don't see that it's any of your business what risks I choose to take with my career!"

Marcel stared at me, white-faced, then turned and strode toward the door.

"Good," I muttered, and sat down to pull off my boots.

But Marcel didn't go. At the door, he hesitated, started out again, hesitated once more, and finally swore, closed and locked the door, and turned back toward me. "All right, Kit," he growled. "I'm risking more than you know telling you this—but damn it, I'm sick and tired of watching Qualls get his hooks into you kids. And after Carstair's Folly..."

"I'm listening," I said, but I kept removing my boots.

"I don't know all of it. But I do know this—none of the Singles Qualls has 'managed' has ever been heard of again."

"Yeah? Well, maybe they didn't have my talent." I finished with the boots and pulled off my shirt.

"Some of them didn't. But some of them did. Some of them had a lot more."

"Hey!" I said, stung.

He ignored me. "And all of them—*all* of them, Kit—were offered gigs on Hydra after their tour ended."

That was news. I stared at him, holding my shirt. "*All* of them?"

"That octopus called The Dealer—it's not the first time I've seen him with Qualls. And there have been other hydras, too."

"Maybe they really like music."

"Maybe. But what happens to the Singles after they go there? They just disappear. I've checked the computer—"

"So have I."

"And found nothing?"

I tossed the shirt aside. "Nada."

"Me either. But whatever is happening to them, Qualls is getting rich from it. You've never seen any of his homes on various planets—but there's no way he's keeping them up on the salary Sensation Singles pays. I should know."

"Maybe he's some kind of meatman."

"I thought of that—but you wouldn't run something like that out in Hydran space. They wouldn't be interested."

I shuddered. "I hope not."

"And then—" Marcel shook his head. "And then there was that business on Carstair's Folly."

"The flashman?"

"Yeah." Marcel sat down on the bed again, hat clutched in both hands. "Kit, you asked me straight out before, and I wouldn't tell you because—well, because I was scared. If Qualls had anything to do with it, he's an even nastier customer than I thought, and if he finds out I've told you all this, or tried to warn you off—"

"I'm not likely to tell him," I said. "But what about the flash-man? Was he—"

"Paris Paradise?"

I nodded.

"It sounds crazy, Kit, and I don't know how it could be true, but—yes. He was."

Something cold crawled into my belly and curled up like it was going to stay for a while. "Flash—"

"Flash ages people, but not like that. It was like—like he'd lived a lifetime in the last two years. And it drove him crazy. Along with the flash."

"And now he's dead."

"Yes."

"Hit by a wheeler."

Marcel nodded.

"Accident?"

Marcel took a deep breath. "I don't think so."

It might not have had anything to do with Qualls, or Hydra, I told myself. *Two years is a long time. Paris Paradise could have been involved in something else we know nothing about...*

But streetsense clobbered me on the side of the head. *I told you to listen to me!* it shouted. *Bad trouble coming. Lift. Lift* now!

I stood up. "You'd better get out of here."

"Right." Marcel stood, put his hat back on, and held out his hand. I shook it. "Good luck, Kit," he said softly. "But watch your back. Qualls is a bad enemy."

"You watch yours." Marcel nodded, crossed to the door, and went out.

I stripped off my mirrortights in a hurry. No shower now—I wanted to be long gone before Qualls came calling. Ignoring my terminal, still flashing furiously at me, I pulled on the same black synthileather pants and microfibre shirt I had donned after Meta dropped in so unexpectedly on Carstair's Folly, then grabbed a bag and hurriedly stuffed it with a few clothes (none of which were mirrorcloth), some souvenirs of the various planets I'd been on, a couple of vidchips of my Single and, of course, my Andy Nebula credit chip. Maybe I could draw off some cash before Qualls shut down my account. I tossed in what little food I had in the kitchen, slung my stringsynth case over my shoulder, and was taking one last look around to make sure I hadn't forgotten anything when the door opened without warning.

"Going somewhere, Kit?" said Qualls.

11

A LITTLE GREEN WAFER

"Yeah," I said, hoping Qualls couldn't hear my heart pounding. "I thought I'd hit the town and sleep somewhere besides this dressing room for a change. Don't worry, I'll be on board long before lift time tomorrow."

"You should have checked with me, first. I told you I'd be by shortly."

"Yeah, well, I didn't want to wait all night."

"I'm afraid you'll have to change your plans. We've decided to lift tonight, instead. The transports are already on their way."

"Oh, come on, Qualls, it's my first time on the old home planet since my Single broke. Can't we spare a day or two?"

"I'm afraid not. Our schedule to Hydra is very tight." Qualls closed the door behind him. "I've come to finalize the plans."

I slowly set my bag down on the floor and the stringsynth beside it. The way Qualls moved, keeping himself between me and the door, holding himself ready to grab me if I tried to dodge past him—to have any chance to escape, I had to make him think I didn't want to. "Great," I said. "Seems to me I've been kept in the dark long enough."

"Good. Sit down."

I complied, sitting on the corner of the bed.

Qualls remained standing. "The Dealer will join us momentarily."

"Orbital," I said, but my stomach fluttered. Getting past Qualls was one thing. Getting past The Dealer...

Qualls glanced at my flashing terminal. "Looks like you still have one fan left, anyway. Or maybe it's some local friend. And you were going to leave without reading it? What was your hurry?"

"I just didn't notice it. I'll read it now." I got up and went to the terminal. Qualls didn't move from his spot by the door. *Taking no chances*, I thought. I turned my back on him and pressed "Retrieve Message."

It appeared only as scrolling words—no video and no audio. Unusual for fan mail; the girls usually wanted to be sure I got a look at their faces. Among other things. "Concert enjoyed greatly, gladeye," it read. "Orbital! But liked music from old days better. Urgent I meet with you before you leave planet. At place we were roomies. I am there tonight. Your gladeye octoman, Rain."

I might have guessed—Rain, again. And this time, there was no doubt he really was on the planet, since he wanted to meet at Fat Sloan's. Maybe that flash of orange I'd seen at the spaceport really had been him. But what was he doing here—and why did he want to meet at Sloan's? I could almost believe our paths crossing by accident in the Pleasure Planets, but on Murdoch IV, in this sludgepool of a city? Coincidence could only explain so much.

I read the message again. It almost sounded like a warning...but, like the warning Marcel had given me, too late.

Way too late. The door opened, and I blanked the screen hurriedly and turned as The Dealer skittered in. No knocking, which mean that not only did Qualls have the access code to my dressing room, he'd given it to The Dealer, too. Throw in Rain's message, and my streetsense practically had me by the throat now. *Get out, get out, get out, lift, lift, lift...*

If only I could. Two more hydras followed The Dealer into the room. I looked at Qualls.

"Business associates," he said smoothly.

I looked back at the two hydras. One stood half a metre taller than the other, with tentacles as big around as my forearm. The smaller one's slender central stalk bent slightly in the middle. Both wore equipment belts. The big hydra's belt held a black rod with a glowing green light at one end—a weapon of some kind, I was willing to bet. The smaller hydra had a flat black case hanging from his belt, about the size of a bookreader. He chitter-squeaked something at The Dealer, who said to Qualls, "All is prepared. Our ship will lift the moment the merchandise—" a tentacle indicated me "—is aboard."

I glared at Qualls. "Merchandise!"

"A minor translation problem," said Qualls. "Please, Kit, sit down." He pointed to the bed. I circled it and sat on the corner again, ready for any chance to dodge past the three hydras and out. Not that it looked likely any chance would present itself. "Dealer, I believe you have a contract for the Hydra engagement?"

The Dealer took a datachip from his belt; Qualls pulled out his handcomp. The Dealer tapped the chip to the side of the comp. Qualls turned the screen toward me. Words were scrolling rapidly across it, too fast to read. They stopped, leaving only a black-bordered square. "Please put your thumbprint here," Qualls said to me.

"Not without reading it."

"It's perfectly standard and in line with our verbal agreement. It binds you for a minimum of six months and a maximum of two years, at your employer's discretion, to perform on a regular basis for Hydra audiences, for which a very sizeable sum will be deposited in your Andy Nebula credit account, with a percentage going to me."

"I said, I'm not thumbing it without reading it!"

Qualls sighed and withdrew the handcomp. "I suppose it was too much to expect you to, but it really would have made things much easier." He glanced at the Dealer.

The Dealer chirped, and the biggest hydra's massive tentacles lashed out at me with the speed of striking snakes, one seizing me around the waist, jerking me upright and spinning me around, one grabbing my left arm and bending it painfully behind me, and a third grabbing my right wrist. I tried to hold my fist closed, but the tentacle tightened inexorably, and Qualls pried my fingers open easily and pressed my thumb to the contract. The handcomp beeped, Qualls tucked it back into the inner breast pocket of his weathercoat, and the big hydra let go of me.

I lunged at Qualls and smashed him to the carpet before the hydras could react. The big one almost yanked my arms out of their sockets as he pulled me back. Qualls picked himself up, rubbing his elbow, and glared at me. "Do it now!" he spat.

The Dealer squealed at the bent-over hydra, and the big one tightened his grip even more. The bent hydra took the black case from his belt and, holding it in one tentacle, opened it with another. Inside, nestled in foam, were three round, silver cylinders. He took one out, closed the case, and unscrewed the cylinder's end. He returned the case to his belt while also gently shaking the cylinder. From it, a thin, bright-green wafer, about two centimetres in diameter, dropped onto the tip of a tentacle.

I stared at it, garish against the hydra's orange skin, the scene spinning as the blood drained from my head. "No..." I wanted to scream it, but it came out in a choked whisper.

"Oh, yes," said Qualls. "I had hoped to put this off until we were in space, but you're becoming far too intractable."

"*No!*" This time I *did* scream it. "Qualls, please, you don't have to—I won't fight any more, I'll go to Hydra—"

"Oh, you will indeed. For two years." He smiled as if at a private joke. "Do you know about hydra memory?" he said conversationally, while that green wafer hovered in front of my face. I had to go cross-eyed to focus on it, but I couldn't look away. "*We* have short-term and long-term memory. *They* have deep memory and surface memory. Everything they see, hear, taste, smell, and feel goes instantly into surface memory— which would quickly overload, if they didn't periodically empty it. So, during what corresponds to our sleep, they sift through the day's events at high speed and consciously decide what they want to keep in surface memory and what they want to shift over to deep memory.

"Everything in surface memory is instantly retrievable.

Deep memories are not, but any experience similar to something in deep memory will instantly bring that deep memory back to the surface. It's like living in a never-ending state of déjà vu. As a result, many hydras, like your old friend Rain, constantly seek unique experiences. It's their major form of entertainment."

Rain. He was waiting for me at Fat Sloan's. He'd come to find out why I didn't show up, wouldn't he?

The wafer moved fractionally closer to my mouth. *Not soon enough*, I thought despairingly. *Not soon enough!*

"But several years ago," Qualls continued, "a Hydran scientist discovered a chemical substance that makes hydras forget. Completely. After taking the drug, a hydra can repeat an experience without being aware of having experienced it before... consciously. Subconsciously, however, there *is* a realization, and the dichotomy between that realization and the complete lack of conscious memory is intensely pleasurable to the hydras, so much so that the drug proved quite addictive.

"Naturally, their government attempted to control this substance, because an addicted hydra eventually sinks to the point of enjoying a handful of experiences over and over again, and quits even trying to do anything new." Qualls actually laughed at that point. "Rather like the fans of Sensation Singles!

"The government's actions drove the drug underground and fostered a criminal trade. Then, hydras met humans. For hydras like The Dealer, this was a very profitable development. Not only did the drug prove to be even more addictive to our kind than to hydras (humans being humans, someone tried it within the first year of contact), we humans waste an enormous amount of intellectual energy on the performing arts, music and dance and theatre, which hydras enjoy almost as much as they enjoy flash.

"Those controlling flash saw the possibilities, and began making human performances available for their customers to experience and, thanks to the drug, re-experience as if for the first time.

"Use of flash skyrocketed. But these enterprising hydras still weren't satisfied. Performances take time—so they decided to do something about *that*, too. They began using an odd side effect of the alternity space drive: the time pocket."

I'd heard of those: self-contained regions of alternity in which time passes differently. Objects or animals placed in one appear to age in minutes instead of weeks or years. I thought of Paris Paradise and blurted in horror, "You can't be serious—"

"Kit, I'm your manager. Would I lie to you? It's such a beautiful blending of technologies. Step into the time pocket, watch the show, take the drug. Watch the show a dozen times if you want, each time as if it's new, each time in greater ecstasy. Step out again to find only a few minutes have passed outside, and your employer and family are none the wiser." He shrugged. "Of course, do it too often and you grow old before your time."

"And the performer?" I whispered.

"Don't all little boys want to grow up faster?"

My heart tried to pound its way through my ribs. "But why *that*?" I pointed my chin at the green wafer.

"Efficiency. The performer—you—has to perform the same number over and over. Flash makes your mind highly receptive to suggestion. We will shape your drug-induced hallucinations so that every time you perform you'll believe you're doing the song for the first time in front of a huge and adoring crowd—

just like tonight. The drug will also give you tremendous energy, which unfortunately heightens the aging effect, but one must sacrifice for one's art. And, of course, flash is instantly and intensely physically addictive, which makes control *so* much easier." He gripped my chin and tilted my head back so I had to look him in the eyes. He smiled. "One other thing. The contract you thumbprinted gives me legal authority to draw on your Andy Nebula credit account, and bequeaths it to me should anything happen to you. So put your mind to rest about where your money will be going—for as long as you have a mind. So far, the cumulative effect of the drug, the time pocket, and endlessly performing the same song has driven every Single insane, some in spectacularly fatal ways." Qualls's smile turned ugly, and he took the green wafer from the tip of the hydra's tentacle. "I look forward to seeing its effect on you." He nodded to The Dealer.

A probing tentacle found my mouth and forced it open. I tried to bite the leathery alien flesh, but my teeth made no impression and I gagged on the bitter taste. And then, Qualls deftly stuck his own finger into my open mouth. The green wafer touched my tongue and instantly dissolved, leaving a faint yeasty taste, and all my resistance dissolved with it.

My body snapped rigid and I fell back onto the bed, staring at the ceiling through a thickening red haze. Fire raced through my veins. Through a deep and increasing roaring I heard Qualls say, his voice two octaves too low, "We'll leave him in here and simply transport the dressing room to your ship."

"This dose is not sufficient for us to begin programming," The Dealer rumbled. "He will require another in space."

"Fine. He's paying for it, anyway."

Their voices whirled away, lost in the roar, which fragmented into other voices, singing voices, a thundering chorus of voices belting out every song I had ever heard.

The initial paralysis left me, and I levitated from the bed, weightlessly bouncing against the ceiling. With just a little more effort I knew I could pass right through it and join those voices, which I now knew were in orbit, only a couple of hundred kilometres straight up...I had power, strength, I could do anything...

I reached out for the energy streaming from the glowtube and wove beams of light around my fingers, changing their colours and flinging them against the walls, laughing as blue and green mixed to cyan, red and blue to magenta, green and red to yellow...

Then the colours whirled together, forming a rainbow maelstrom I could no longer control. The colours darkened, deepened into thick, inky black, blinding me. The thunder of the whirlpool drowned out the voices. It sucked me in, swallowed me., and then spat me out again onto a wet Fistfight City street, beneath a garish green holosign, wearing nothing but thin pyjamas. I was cold, I was hungry—and small, so small.

No! I screamed. *I don't want to be back here!* But I looked up and read the sign even though I didn't want to: "Deep Love Orphanage." Then my gaze went lower, to the sliding metal gate, standing ajar, and I knew I had just short-circuited the Gatekeeper and escaped, and I knew I had to run because I could hear the alarms ringing inside and they'd be after me, but my feet wouldn't move, and I looked down and saw that I didn't *have* feet, I had orange crablegs like a hydra's, and my legs had joined into a stalk, and my arms were twisting into tentacles, and I opened my mouth to scream but all that came out was an alien shriek that echoed back from the walls of the orphanage as insane laughter…

…and then I was lying on the bed in my dressing room again, shaking and shivering and sweating, and Meta was leaning over me.

Another hallucination, I thought dimly. *She'll turn into something horrible in a minute.*

But she stayed the same girl she'd always been. "Kit, are you all right? I saw Qualls and those other—things—come out, but when I knocked you didn't answer. I was afraid you were sick…"

It couldn't be Meta. "Door…locked…"

Meta grinned. "I have one of Mr. Qualls's all-access keycards."

It *definitely* couldn't be Meta. "You could—couldn't—"

"I stole it at the hotel. He tried to lock me in my room."

I managed to raise myself up. "Got to—got to go—"

"No," Meta said firmly. "Lie down. You're sick—"

"Not sick…drugged." I could feel reality slipping away, voices and monsters gibbering in my mind, and I clutched her arms, desperate to feel something solid. "Qualls. Help me—"

"All right, all right." Meta looked around, spotted my bag and stringsynth, and grabbed both. "Can you walk?"

"Have—to—" Clinging to her, I made it as far as the door, while the dressing room turned inside-out in my head and Meta sprouted green leaves. "Get us out—the streets—we can hide there." *Fat Sloan's,* I thought. *Rain. Maybe he can help…*

"Just like in your song!" Meta almost squealed.

"Only—you're rescuing *me*," I said, and hoped, as we stepped out into the misty night, that it was true.

1 2

RATS ON THE RUN

FLASH IS CALLED flash because it acts instantly (as I'd already discovered) and because its effects recur over and over, like the flashing of a light, until it's eliminated from the body. For the next few hours, I'd be out of my mind more than I was in it—and might not always know the difference.

Meta headed for the gate. "Qualls—" I said, resisting.

"The security people come with the stadium, don't they?"

Did they? Yeah, they did. I nodded.

"Then just leave it to me."

I didn't have much choice. Neither my brain nor my body were exactly at their best. Only my arm around Meta's shoulders kept me upright.

A frowning security guard met us at the gate. "Passes?"

"I'm with him," Meta said sweetly, and I managed to lift my head. The guard shone a flashlight in my face. His eyes widened.

"Sorry, Mr. Nebula—"

"Oh, label me Andy, gladeye," I said. "Everyone else does... did...didee-da-dit-da-dit..." My words turned into phosphorescent balloons, and I waved good-bye as they lifted into the sky.

The guard looked up, then back down at me. "Is he all right?" His voice started three octaves below middle C and screeched to a high C-sharp in the space of four words. I winced.

"Should be a singer, gladeye! What a range...range...range, range on the home..." The guard sprouted bovine horns.

"He's just—happy," Meta said. "Happy to be home. We're going out celebrating!"

"Looks to me like he's already been celebrating," the guard said. "Well, enjoy yourself, Mr.—Andy."

"Moo! Moooo!" I said to him, and suddenly everything snapped back to normal...or near-normal. I straightened abruptly. "Thank you very much, kind sir."

Then I turned to Meta. "I'll take my stringsynth now, my dear."

She raised an eyebrow at my suddenly grand tone, but handed me the long, slender case. I slung its strap over my shoulder so the stringsynth rested on my back, then took my bag from her. Holding it in my right hand, I offered her my left arm. "Shall we go, milady?"

With an elegant inclination of her head to indicate acceptance, she hooked her arm in mine, and in that fashion, we processed grandly down the street—

—right up until a clamour abruptly arose from the stadium and the guard's communicator squawked.

"Uh-oh," I said.

"What's going on?"

Meta started to turn around, just as the guard shouted, "Stop! Mr. Nebula, stop!"

I grabbed Meta's hand. "Run!"

"A minute ago you couldn't even walk!" Meta protested above the thudding of our feet on the pavement.

Sirens wailed from somewhere ahead. "Police—and ambulance!" I shouted. "Faster!" My blood blazed anew, filling me with energy. *This* was what flash was all about! I ran as fast as I could, almost dragging Meta, laughing out loud as shockwaves of colour exploded around us. Green fire burned in our wake, silver stars burst from our mouths and drifted to the ground like snow—

The flash ended. "Kit, stop! Stop!" Meta screamed.

I stopped. Meta broke free and stumbled away from me, sobbing, clutching her arm, and I saw my handprint outlined in red on her skin. "What's *wrong* with you? What's going on?"

The manic energy had vanished. I felt weak, sick—and lost. I stared around. How far had we run? Blank brick walls surrounded us. I could still hear the sirens, slowing, fading, back at the stadium. "Meta, I'm sorry! I didn't mean to—it's the drug—"

"What drug? I thought—a sedative, to knock you out—"

"No..." My knees gave out and I sat down abruptly on the curb, my bag in the gutter beside me. "No, Meta. He—" I took a deep breath. "He gave me flash."

Her hands flew to her mouth. "Kit, no!"

I nodded miserably. "And that's not all...I can't go back, Meta. I've got to hide from him, hide until he gives up."

Meta sat down on the curb beside me. "Then I can't, either!"

"What?" Awful realization hit me. "Oh, Meta—I'm sorry, I

didn't—" Rage suddenly exploded in me like a volcano, rage at my stupidity and blindness. I roared my anger and self-loathing at the top of my lungs, pounding my thighs with my fists—then I raised my hands high over my head, screaming, and brought them down as claws to rake at my face—

—and something stopped me, some force that dared to stand against my fury. My anger, coiled under my skin like vicious, poisonous, black snakes, suddenly lashed out at whatever it was that dared to thwart my—

And then the flash passed, and I found myself standing over Meta, fingers clawed, her hands holding my wrists. I jerked free of her and stumbled back, dragging the back of my hand across my froth-flecked lips. "Meta...I can't...you've got to leave, get away from me. I was going to...I could have..."

"I've got nowhere to go," Meta cried. "You know this city, I don't. And if I go back to Qualls—if he's as bad as you say—"

"But I—" I covered my face with my hands, took a deep breath and tried to control the shaking. The flash was a time bomb in my blood. The first dose hits hardest, I'd heard that often enough...but how hard? How long? Yet Meta was right. I couldn't leave her, she wouldn't last six hours on the street, and I couldn't send her back to Qualls. He'd take her hostage to try to force me back.

I'd gotten her into this, I had to get her out. I leaned against the nearest wall. "I'm all right for the moment. The lucid periods should last longer and longer, and I've never heard of a dose lasting longer than a few hours." And after that? How long before I began craving the next dose? Well, one problem at a time. "Just...watch me. If I start acting strange, stay clear until —until it's over."

"But what if you try to hurt yourself again?"

"Let me," I said bitterly.

"Don't be stupid!"

The words came out like a verbal slap. I took a deep breath. "Sorry."

She came closer. "So, where will we go? "

"Fat Sloan's. It's a flop—um, a hotel. A friend sent me a message to meet him there."

"Can you trust him?"

I opened my mouth to say "yes"—and stopped. *Could* I trust Rain? I hardly knew him. And he was a hydra, like The Dealer. My earlier doubts, about whether he had somehow arranged my initial meeting with Qualls, came flooding back. Maybe he was a friend of The Dealer's. Maybe he'd sent that message just to ensure that, even if I escaped the stadium, I'd still run straight into their clutches. Qualls had made a point of telling me I had a message waiting…

Damn it. "Maybe not. So forget Fat Sloan's. We'll just hole up around here until I'm—normal. Then I'm putting you on the first ship to Carstair's Folly."

"Kit—"

"No arguments. Qualls is dangerous—and right now, so am I. I'm getting you away. Then I'll only only have myself to worry about."

"But they gave you *flash*, Kit. You're going to need help—"

"My problem. Not yours."

Her lips pressed together. She didn't look like I'd convinced her, but she jerked an angry nod.

"Good. Now…" I didn't know *exactly* where we were, but I knew the neighbourhood. No good for street-singing, but not bad for hiding. I used to have three or four "addresses" in this district—mostly abandoned warehouses. All I needed was a signpost. Retrieving my bag from the gutter, I started up the street.

Meta watched me carefully as we splashed along the potholed pavement. "Are you—normal, right now?" she said finally.

My heart skipped a beat. "I think so," I said cautiously.

"Just checking." She shrugged. "It's hard to tell, with you."

I laughed and took a playful swipe at her head. "Why you—"

She danced out of reach and I ran after her, and for a few seconds, as we played tag, I forgot everything else—

—right up until the 'forcer car slowly rounded the corner far behind us. I saw it first and lunged at Meta. "Meta—"

"You sure are slow for such a great dancer—" she taunted, then must have seen something in my eyes, because she stopped and followed my gaze. "Maybe you could just tell them about Qualls...?" she said doubtfully.

I shook my head. "Not with flash in my blood. That's a crime right there. Run!" I dashed down the street. Maybe they hadn't seen us...

They had. Infrared nightsight, probably. I heard the whine of a powerful electric motor and suddenly the whole front of the car lit up with blinding light, making the street brighter than day—and showing us only too clearly there was nowhere to hide.

But it also revealed street signs up ahead: Warehouse Road Four and Thrustfire Boulevard. My heart leaped. "Got it!" I cried. "Come on!"

We reached the corner with the 'forcers half a block behind

but gaining fast. I dragged Meta out of the light and across Thrustfire, then dodged immediately down a narrow space between two buildings. We reached another alley, parallel to Thrustfire, just as the police car squealed around the corner. As we ducked into the cross-alley the flash of a spotlight speared the space between the buildings where we'd just been. "I've still got my old timing," I said gleefully. "Who's slow?"

"Don't stop!" Meta cried, tugging at my hand.

"Not that way. This way!" Back into the narrow slot between the buildings we went. The whine of the 'forcers' car slowed and stopped; a door unlatched. "They'll be down here any second," I whispered, stooping over and searching the base of the building on the right. "This place had better still be —got it!"

"Got what?"

I bent down to a small basement window. It looked boarded-up, but in fact the boards, attached to each other and hinged at the top, lifted like a trap door, revealing a black rectangle, the window glass having long since vanished. A musty smell wafted out into the alley. I tossed my bag through the opening, unslung the stringsynth case and lowered it in more carefully, and then turned to Meta. "After you."

She hesitated. "It's dark."

"Well, wait a sec and the 'forcers will light it up for you—"

Without another word she lowered herself through and disappeared. I sat down, poked my legs into the basement, slid through the window—and stuck. My heart raced. Eight months —I'd grown— "Pull!" I whispered fiercely to Meta, and felt her grab my legs and tug on them. I pushed against the pavement with all my strength.

Footsteps echoed from the street. The 'forcers would shine a light down here in a minute and find me, half in and half out, caught like a rat—

I felt myself transform, my clothes turning to grey fur, my face elongating, sprouting whiskers, my teeth growing long and sharp. I could smell the humans around the corner, smell their sweat and the sharp metallic scent of their horrible rat-killing clubs, and I wriggled frantically and suddenly was free, leaving fur and skin behind but dropping into wonderful darkness. Quick as thought I turned around and closed the jaws of the trap. An instant later light flashed across the gaps in the boards, and then came the heavy tread of the humans passing by, never knowing the rats they sought were close enough to bite them.

The little rat sharing my hole squeaked at me. Ignoring her, I curled myself up nose to tail and went blissfully to sleep.

13

REUNION

THE NEXT MORNING, I was more-or-less myself, except for a badly scraped shoulder beneath a ragged tear in my shirt. But I didn't know how long it would last. With Meta still protesting that she wanted to stay with me, I set out for the spaceport.

"I don't know who Qualls and the hydras have looking for us," I told Meta as we emerged, blinking in the morning light, onto still-deserted Thrustfire Boulevard. "For all I know, there are 'forcers on Qualls's payroll. That means back alleys and zigzags, all the way. Stay close."

"Don't worry," Meta said. I looked at her dirty clothes and face and bedraggled hair, and knew I must look just as bad. *Good-bye Andy Nebula, interstellar rock star, hello streetslug Kit.*

The trip took half a day. More than once we dodged 'forcers, ducking into dark alleyways that stank of garbage and human waste, slipping down narrow passages I used to fit through easily that were now barely wide enough, hiding behind gutted vehicles. As we neared downtown, more and more transports and personal vehicles crowded the streets. The people filling the sidewalks didn't give us a second glance after the first one of contempt. "It's like they don't even see us!" Meta complained, after one particularly overdressed female passed us by. "Can't they tell we're in trouble, that we need help?"

"They see people like us all the time." I pointed to a grey-haired woman slumped in a doorway. "If they tried to help us, they might have to help everyone. They're busy people; they don't have the time. Besides, we don't *want* any notice, remember?"

"I guess not." Meta glared at another woman, who quickened her steps. "But I don't like being treated like something a dog left behind."

I shrugged. Nothing had made me feel more at "home" than the way that woman's eyes had flicked past me. Andy Nebula was only skin deep. Under that skin was Kit.

And under Kit's skin was flash. I said nothing to Meta, but I could feel it working away, bursts of tingling travelling from fingertips to spine, phantom itches appearing and disappearing. Less than a day after my first dose, and…

I licked dry lips. And I wanted more. Right now that was all it was—want—but I knew in a few short hours it would be more than want; it would be need.

I had to get Meta away before then. I began to take more risks, crossing streets at main intersections, counting on the growing crowds to hide us from passing 'forcers. Finally, the glass-and-steel facade of the spaceport terminal came into sight, and I stopped long enough to open my bag and take out Andy Nebula's credit chip. "I don't want to linger," I said to Meta. "We go in, I buy your ticket," (*if this thing still works*, I thought), "and you head for the departure lounge—I don't care how long it is until you lift. You'll be safe in there."

"What about you?"

"Don't worry about me. I can look after myself."

Meta said nothing, but looked skeptical.

Down the street, across another, and into the terminal building. Holosigns competed with vidscreens for attention. An old man sat playing a stringsynth—badly—his case open at his feet. Meta in tow, I sought departure information. A vidscreen sensed me passing and burst into life. "Andy Nebula!" it yelled.

I froze and stared at it. My face filled the screen as the voice-over continued, "...the Murdoch IV-born teenaged Sensation Single who performed for 30,000 screaming fans at Brankston Memorial Stadium last night, today is on the run. He's the prime suspect in the murder of Marcel Roy, forty-six, standard, his stage manager, who was knifed backstage shortly after the concert. Nebula's manager, Samuel Qualls, told 'forcers Nebula and Roy had come close to blows on more than one occasion. Their dispute may have been drug-related, Qualls said; Nebula is a flash-user and Roy may have been his supplier..."

I grabbed Meta and hurried her away, ducking into a short hallway leading to a cleaning-supply room. Meta shook free and backed away, staring at me. "You don't believe that, do you?" I cried. "I didn't kill Roy. And I'm not a flash-user, either!" *Or wasn't*, I thought bitterly. "Meta, Marcel came to warn me. He told me to get away before Qualls came—but I didn't make it. Qualls knew I was trying to run, he must have guessed Marcel had warned me, and—" I shook my head at the sick cleverness of it all. "He killed Marcel, made me the suspect, and told them I'd run off, all the while thinking I was locked in my dressing room. He would have smuggled me off to Hydra and no one would have ever known what had happened to me. I would have just dropped out of sight. But you messed things up for him by helping me disappear for real." I looked at the credit chip in my hand. "As soon as I use this, the 'forcers will know. They'll find me in minutes."

"Let them!" Meta cried. "Tell them the truth. Turn yourself in. At least you'll be in their hands and not Qualls's."

It made sense, now I knew the 'forcers weren't working for Qualls—though it was a hard pill to swallow for an old street-slug. "You're right. But first, you're getting out of here."

Meta nodded. "I think I'm ready to go home now," she said in a small voice. "In your Single, street life seemed so...romantic."

"I know," I said. "And it's not. It's dirty and hard and sometimes very short. And you've only seen the surface, Meta. You haven't seen the worst parts of this city, or the worst people."

"Except Qualls."

"Except Qualls. He's as bad as they come." I could hear the newsvid blaring my story again. "Let's get out of here."

I found a bank of screens displaying departures to the Pleasure Planets; there was one late that evening. I memorized the ship number and headed for the appropriate ticket counter.

I'd lost my edge, living as Andy Nebula, or I would have seen them leaning against the mirrored pillars long before I did. I grabbed Meta's arm again. "Stand very still."

Like one of my flash-induced hallucinations, a young man in mirrorcloth materialized in front of me. He was thinner, and the white of his eyes had begun to grey, but his smile was as nasty as ever. "Hey, flashmates," he drawled. "Scan who's back in our orbit."

Meta drew closer to me. "Who—"

"They label me Dry Ice, little double-X. Maybe this street-slime you're with has told you about me."

"Kit?"

I squeezed her hand reassuringly, and wished someone would do the same for me. "What's powering, Dry Ice?" I didn't have to turn around to know the rest of the Ice Boys were surrounding me.

"You've been playing with radwaste, gladeye. High-level. Our flashsource says we take you, he'll power us all for a month." Dry Ice shrugged. "So we take you, gladeye. Or is that Mr. Nebula?"

He hadn't activated his forceblade; he was counting on his mates. They were all behind me, blocking the way to the exits—

—to the *legal* exits.

"No need to call me Mr. Nebula, gladeye." I turned to Meta, and held out my bag. Her eyes met mine, and maybe I managed a little telepathy, because they widened and her knuckles whitened on the bag's straps as she took it. I faced Dry Ice again. "I'm only Andy Nebula when I'm dancing. Like this!"

The move was the climax of my Single, the high, spinning leap that ended with a snap of my foot into the chest of the dancebot playing the leader of the enemy flashgang. Every time I'd performed it, I'd imagined Dry Ice on the receiving end. His eyes barely had time to widen before my foot smashed into him and sent him flying back, tumbling over a pile of luggage.

I grabbed Meta and, with the Ice Boys in pursuit, dashed straight toward the ticket desk. We smashed through the line in a flurry of screams, scrambled madly over the desk itself, charged through the door beyond into another room, and crashed through the door at the back of that into the huge cargo-sorting facility.

To our left I saw daylight, and like a trapped animal I headed for it instinctively, leaping over conveyor belts, almost dragging Meta. Seconds later we burst out of a fire exit into the street, running for our lives.

Behind us came the Ice Boys.

1 4

FAT SLOAN SAVES THE DAY

WE DIDN'T HAVE MUCH of a head start, and we couldn't hope to outrun them. Still, we ran, crashing into and over pedestrians who swore at us, then saw the Ice Boys coming and scrambled out of the way. Instinctively I headed for my home territory, the dozen or so square blocks I knew best. But I couldn't duck into any of my hidey-holes with the Ice Boys breathing down my neck.

"I—can't—" Meta panted.

"You've got to!" I shouted. Dry Ice needed me in good shape to hand over to Qualls, but he probably had no orders at all about Meta, and if the Ice Boys got hold of her... "Just—a little farther."

I was hoping for a miracle—and I got it. We pounded around a corner and toward Fat Sloan's. For a few seconds we were out of sight of the Ice Boys, but Fat Sloan's would be no refuge—

Except there stood Fat Sloan himself, filling the doorway. "Quick, Kit, in here," he said, and stepped aside.

Any port in a storm, I thought, and ducked through, Meta close behind. The moment we were in the dingy lobby, Sloan moved back into the doorway, effectively blocking it. I pushed Meta down behind the counter and crouched beside her. She dropped my bag on the floor between us.

Just in time. "You see streetslime flowing by here, gladeye?" Dry Ice demanded of Sloan.

"A boy and a girl just passed. Turned left at the corner."

"More thrust, flashmates!" Dry Ice shouted. Footsteps clattered away.

I stayed put, the handle of a floor safe digging into my knee, until Fat Sloan loomed over us. "They're gone."

"Gratitudes, gladeye." I helped Meta up. "Our friend here is labelled Fa—Sloan," I told her.

"My pleasure," said Sloan, holding out one greasy hand.

Meta accepted it gingerly and let go almost at once. "Thank you for hiding us, Mr. Sloan."

"Anything for an old friend like Kit."

"How did you know we were running this way?" I asked him.

"This." He tapped a control pad on the desk and four tiny vidscreens flickered to life, showing the streets outside. On one of them, the Ice Boys fanned out down a garbage-strewn alley. "I like to see trouble before it gets here." He grinned, a frightening sight. "Besides, I've been expecting you. You're late."

"Huh?"

"Your hydra friend told me you would be here last night. He seemed most perturbed when you didn't show up."

Rain! "Is he still here?" *Is this a trap?*

"No. He left early this morning. " Sloan pulled a keyrod out of a drawer. "Here. The room's free for tonight."

"What if Dry Ice comes back? He might want to search the place."

Sloan pulled something else out of the drawer, something flat black, with a handle and a short barrel: a (highly illegal) slugthrower. "He won't."

I nodded, and took the keychip. "This way, " I said to Meta. I grabbed my bag, and we headed for the stairs.

"Wait!" Sloan called after us. When I turned back, he tossed four mealpacs my way. "On the house."

"Thanks, Sloan." I led Meta to the room—the same room I had shared with Rain. I wondered if Sloan remembered that.

Heaving a shaking sigh, Meta sat on the bed and then flopped onto her back. She put her forearm over her eyes. "I don't like your world. And I don't like your friends."

"I don't like it, either. And I don't have any friends here." I tossed my bag into the corner the farthest from the door, and unslung the stringsynth case and leaned it against the wall. Then I opened one of the mealpacs. The savoury smell reminded me just how hungry I really was, and brought Meta upright again, swallowing. I handed her the one I'd opened and took another for myself, then sat in the only chair by the little table to eat it.

"Sloan—" Meta began as she freed her spoon from the packaging.

"He's not my friend. He never offered me a free room in the old days when I needed it just as bad, that's for sure." I dug into the steaming stew inside the pac.

"Then why—?"

"I don't know." *And I don't like it,* I thought, but all I could really think about was the food. I hadn't had anything to eat since before the concert, and a lot had happened since then.

Meta, too, remained silent as we ate, but I could tell she was thinking over what I'd said. "Maybe he's planning to call the 'forcers," she said at last.

I snorted. "Sloan? He'd sooner go jogging."

Meta stared at me for a minute, then giggled, the sound taking me back to the day she'd sneaked into my dressing room. My last mouthful lost its taste. *Look what being my fan has gotten her into.* "That I'd like to see," she said.

"I wouldn't. Could cause earthquakes."

That set her off again.

"And what if he fell in the river? Floods!"

It was good to hear her laugh, but I couldn't keep it up. For one thing, I ran out of Sloan jokes. For another, I was too busy wondering what Sloan was really up to. Would he try to sell us to the Ice Boys? No—he hated flashgangs. But—

And suddenly, I understood. "Got it!"

"Got what?" Meta said around a mouthful of stew.

"What Sloan's up to. He's planning to sell us to Qualls."

Meta's eyes widened. "Then hadn't we better—"

"He won't do it right away," I said, thinking out loud. "He thinks we're safely tucked away and unsuspecting, so he won't be in a hurry. And he won't tell Qualls we're *here,* or Qualls might send the Ice Boys to come get us and Sloan would have to face them in earnest. No. He'll call Qualls, plan a meeting, set up a place to hand us over. We've probably got until morning."

Meta sighed and sat back again. She pushed her hair back

with the hand that wasn't holding a spoon. "Good. I don't think I could run another step."

"And, of course," I went on, "we won't be here."

She groaned. "More running? More hiding in basements? Anyone you meet could recognize you. Sooner or later, Qualls will catch you."

"If I'm still on the planet."

"If you try to buy passage with your credchip, they'll nail you. You said so yourself."

"Who said anything about buying passage?" I pointed at her. "As you should know, there are other ways to get off a planet."

"Stow away?" Meta blinked, then grinned. "I like it!"

"I thought you would." I yawned. "If I were you, I'd get some sleep. In fact, I'm not you, and I'm going to get some sleep anyway." I leaned back in the chair and stretched out my legs. "We'll have to sneak out in the middle of the night..."

"I *could* use a nap," Meta admitted. She started to lie back, hesitated, leaned over and sniffed the dingy covers, got up, pulled the bedspread to the bottom, and instead lay down on the sheets. (I doubted they were much cleaner, but I didn't blame her for trying.) Within seconds, her even breathing and the slow rise and fall of her chest told me she slept.

I immediately sat up straight again. I'd lied; I couldn't sleep. Jittery energy filled me, along with a growing hunger I knew eating couldn't cure, a hunger like a deep itch that couldn't be scratched. *Flashwish.* And it was just beginning.

All my plans would be useless if I couldn't control it. It could make me do something stupid or reckless. What I feared most was that it would make me beg Sloan for flash. I knew he sold it. All I had to do was ask and he'd open up that little safe and take out a vial filled with small green wafers...

Already the idea tempted my body, teased my mind. I got to my feet and started pacing. *Ignore it,* I told myself. *Plan how you're going to stow away.*

Meta had shown me the easiest way—sneak into a cargo module. But we'd have to be very careful. Not all modules were pressurized, and neither were some holds. At least the destination didn't matter—anywhere off Murdoch IV would suit me, anywhere I could talk freely to the authorities and the media about what Qualls had been up to.

I found myself almost running from wall to wall. I forced myself to slow, then to sit down; then I hopped up again, grabbed the soap and the thin, worn towel by the sink, and went down the hallway to the bathroom that served the whole floor. I thought a shower might make me feel better.

It didn't. I came back to the room damp, clean—a lot cleaner than the shower itself had been—and hurting. Meta half-woke as I came in, but rolled over and went immediately back to sleep. I sat down and clenched my fists and resolved not to move from that chair, no matter how bad it got.

It was a resolution I couldn't keep. I dozed, but then woke with a gasp, heart racing, body soaked in sweat. Pain stabbed my right elbow, skewered my left knee. I moaned. Meta mumbled something, then sat up, blinking sleepily, and said, "Kit...?"

"Go back to sleep," I said—but then couldn't suppress a grunt as agony flared in my left wrist. Meta sat up straighter.

"What is it? What's wrong?"

"Flash—"

She pushed herself away from me, pressing her back against the wall. "You said it was gone!"

I laughed, a little wildly. "Oh, it's gone, all right. That's the problem." I doubled over as pain bludgeoned me in the stomach. "This," I groaned, "is withdrawal."

Meta pulled her knees up against her chest. "What can I do?"

I'd had no idea it would be this bad. And it had only begun. I couldn't beat it; I knew that now. Not on my own.

"Find something—to tie me up with," I gasped out. "Tie me to the chair. Don't let me up—whatever happens. Unh!"

"Kit, I can't—"

"Do it!" I screamed. She stared at me, eyes wide, then scrambled off the bed, stripped the sheet from it, and tore the sheet into four long strips, while I hunched over in the chair, rocking with pain. Tears streamed down my face. "Hurry!"

"I'm hurrying!" She grabbed my arms and lashed each one to the chair, did the same with my legs, then backed away from me again as though I might turn into something horrible.

I might. "You don't have to watch—" My throat squeezed closed, choking off the words.

"I can't—I won't leave you!"

"You won't like it."

"Neither will you!"

She was right.

15

WITHDRAWAL

THE PAIN GREW until I couldn't stand it—and then grew more. It flayed the skin from my body and the flesh from my bones, poured acid through my veins, drove slivers of ice into my eyes, filled my throat with ground glass. And all the time I knew exactly what I needed to end the agony: one little wafer, one insignificant, unimportant wafer, one tiny dose of flash.

I writhed and screamed, spittle dribbling down my chin. I begged Meta until I was hoarse, "Please, let me up! I've got to find—I have to have—" But Meta buried her face in the pillow, her hands over her ears.

After what seemed days, but was probably less than an hour, Fat Sloan opened the door. Adrenalin surged through me. "Sloan, you can get me flash, I know you can, Sloan, please, please!"

Meta's head jerked up. "No!"

Sloan ignored her and came over to me. "Well," he said. "So little Kit, always so afraid of flashmen, is a flashman himself."

"Sloan..." I moaned. "Help me..."

"Of course, gladeye." Sloan drew a glass tube out of his shirt pocket and shook a little green wafer into his palm.

I trembled and drooled like a starving mutt. "Thank you, Sloan," I whispered, like a prayer. "Thank you, thank you—"

"Don't mention it." Sloan delicately took the wafer between his grimy thumb and forefinger and leaned forward. "Open wide—"

I opened my mouth, tongue extended, panting in short little gasps, waiting for the blessed touch of the wafer—

And Meta screamed "Stop!" and threw herself between us. The wafer spun away, smashing to green dust against the wall.

Sloan's smile turned to snarl. "I'm just giving him what he wants—what they all want!" he spat. "You can't stop me."

"Meta, get out of his way!"

She ignored me. "I won't let you do it!"

Sloan laughed, a nasty sound. "I don't think you can stop me." He stepped forward again, a moving mountain of flesh.

But Meta held her ground. "I won't let you," she repeated—and held up the knife I'd put in my bag. She handled it clumsily, but it was very long and very sharp, and Sloan stopped. The sight of it filled me with rage. How dare she use *my* knife to stop Sloan from giving me what I needed? Who'd asked her to interfere?

Sloan snorted. "Have it your way, little girl. But don't expect him to thank you for it." He went out, slamming the door.

Meta turned toward me with a grin—and I spat at her and called her every obscene name I had learned on the street. "I'll kill you!" I screamed. "You're biowaste, you filthy little witch!

I'll take that knife and—" I went into graphic detail, punctuated by my own moans and gasps when pain crashed over me.

My words drove Meta back against the wall, her knees pulled up tight, but she didn't hide her face this time—she just stared at me, rocking back and forth, tears running down her cheeks.

A century later, the pain ebbed, and consciousness with it.

———

I WOKE IN DARKNESS. Every bone and muscle ached, sandpaper lined my throat, and I stank. But I could think clearly again.

Meta slept, curled up on the bed like a cat, a faint glitter of reflected light from the tavern holosign across the road showing the knife still lying by her outstretched hand. I shook my head. *Little Meta, standing up to Fat Sloan on my account. Now that's what I call a fan.* I opened my mouth and croaked, "Meta." She didn't stir. "Meta, wake up!"

"Mmmm?" She rolled over, then suddenly sat up and stared at me, her eyes wide and white in the darkness. "Kit?"

"Yes. It's over. You can let me go."

She didn't move. "How can I be sure?" she whispered.

I opened my mouth to say, *Don't be silly, you can be sure because I'm telling you*—but the words stuck in my throat. I had to swallow hard before I could speak. "I'm sorry, Meta. I'm so sorry." Remembering the names I had called her, I wanted to sink through the floor. "That wasn't me talking—it was the flash."

"You said you'd kill me."

"Meta, it's late, and we've got to get out of here tonight, before Sloan hands us over to Qualls. If you don't untie me, they'll catch me—and they'll put me back on flash again first thing. And then all this will have been for nothing."

She hesitated a moment longer, then grabbed the knife, sliced through the cloth strips tying me to the chair, and stepped back warily, holding her weapon at the ready in case I leaped at her.

I couldn't have leaped from that chair if it had been on fire. Every movement hurt. Very slowly, I straightened my stiffened legs and managed to stand, then hobbled over to the door and turned on the light. I surveyed myself in the cracked mirror—not a pretty sight. Dried blood and spit covered my blotchy face and the front of my torn synthileather shirt. Slowly and painfully I pulled it off, washed as best I could in the sink, then towelled off and limped over to my bag for a clean shirt—simple white cloth this time. Meta watched me, never lowering the knife. When I'd finished, I held out my hand. "I think I should carry that."

For a moment she didn't move; then, abruptly, she held it out to me, hilt-first. I took it. "You were very brave," I said.

"I couldn't let you take that stuff, not after...what I'd seen."

"Would you have actually used the knife on him?" I held it up and turned it so the blade flashed in the light. "*Could* you do something like that?"

"I—I think I could. To protect a friend." Her mouth quirked. "Anyway, *he* sure thought I could."

To protect a friend. I thought again of what I had called her, of everything she'd been through because of me. *Some friend.* Ashamed to look at her, I slid the knife into its sheath and put the sheath on my belt, then closed the bag, picked it up—and stopped, reconsidering. Nothing in it was really important, and I could do without the weight. I opened it again, took out my Andy Nebula credchip, put it in my shirt pocket, and kicked the bag under the bed.

Then I picked up the stringsynth in its worn, black case and slung it on my back. The battered old instrument wasn't worth anything, but it had been with me from the beginning and I didn't want to leave it behind, even though it weighed me down. "Orbital," I said. "Our next trick is getting past Fat Sloan."

"Won't he be asleep?"

"His security systems won't. He doesn't like people coming and going without him knowing. Especially us. We're worth money."

"So how do we get out?"

"I'm not sure yet." I looked at the window, toying with the idea of turning the rest of the sheet into a rope, but thought better of it. The tavern across the street would still be full of people and we didn't want a crowd of witnesses.

So if we couldn't go down—we'd have to go up. "The roof."

I turned off the light, eased the door open, and peered both ways. It was unusually quiet, for Sloan's; nobody arguing or screaming. I slipped out, Meta behind me, and crept to the stairs as silently as the rickety old floor would let me. Dim yellow light shone into the stairwell from the lobby; I wondered if Sloan was down there, overflowing that stool of his.

I wasn't about to go down to find out. Instead, we crept up, step by creaking step. I expected every minute to see Sloan appear at the bottom of the stairs, blocking out the light like an eclipsing moon, but everything remained quiet. Two flights up, the stairs ended in a red metal door with no handle. A single dim glowtube barely lit it.

"Dead end?" Meta glanced down the stairs.

"No," I said. The door might be steel—but its wooden frame looked as rotten as Sloan's heart. "Stand back."

I braced myself against the stair railing and kicked as hard as I could. The door crashed open, splinters flying, and somewhere below us a piercing *beep! beep! beep!* began. "Oops," I said. I grabbed Meta's hand and we ran out onto the flat, gravel-covered roof, toward the two red railings, curving over the knee-high wooden wall girdling the rooftop, that marked the fire escape leading down into the back alley.

I glanced back as we reached it. Sloan *had* been in the lobby; he appeared, puffing, in the shattered doorway, illegal slugthrower in his hand. He raised it. "Stop!" he shouted.

"I don't think so," I yelled back.

The slugthrower cracked and spat fire, and a large chunk of the wooden wall exploded in splinters, one of which scored my cheek, bringing a warm trickle of blood. "Next time I won't miss!" Sloan shouted.

"Go!" I told Meta. She grabbed the railings, heaved herself up and over the wall, turned, and started down the ladder on the other side.

He won't really shoot me, I thought. *He needs me alive.*

Crack! Another slug whined past, so close my insides quivered.

I hope. I grabbed the fire-escape railings, put my foot on top of the wooden wall, pushed myself up—

—and the gun cracked one more time.

Something smashed into my back.

I tumbled forward into empty space.

16

STOWAWAYS

"KIT!" Meta screamed.

I probably would have screamed, too, if my breath hadn't been knocked out when my foot caught between the topmost rung and the wall and I smashed hard against the outside of the fire escape. I hung there, gasping soundlessly for air, dangling by one leg over three stories of darkness, expecting at any moment to feel the beginning of pain from the bullet wound, or blood running down past my face.

But I didn't. Oh, there was plenty of pain, not just from my back, where whatever-it-was had hit me, but also from my abused ankle, my bruised chest and face, my scraped shoulder, my bleeding cheek, and everything in between. None of it felt like it a gunshot wound, though...or how I imagined a gunshot wound would feel.

I tried to pull myself back up and couldn't. "Meta, help!"

"You're alive!"

"I won't be if you don't give me a hand!" I could feel my foot slipping. "Hurry!"

With her help and a pulled muscle or two I managed to get a safe grip on the outside of the fire escape, free my foot, and swing around onto the first landing, where the fire escape changed from a ladder to a series of switchbacking staircases. Sitting there, I unslung the stringsynth case from my back and confirmed what I'd suspected: Sloan's slug, whether because he was a good shot or a spectacularly bad one, had indeed hit me square in the back—but my poor old stringsynth, heavy, old, and almost solid metal, had saved my life. Maybe luck hadn't completely deserted me after all.

Feeling guilty, as if I were abandoning an old friend, I left the ruined instrument on the landing, pulled myself to my feet, said, "Come on!", took two steps down—and stopped so suddenly Meta ran into me.

"Now what?" she cried.

"Sloan's not here."

"Good! Now go!"

"But he should be here—all he had to do was cross the roof. That means—" I climbed back to the top of the fire escape and raised my head slowly over the edge of the roof. No Sloan. "This way! He thinks I fell—he must be heading for the bottom of the fire escape!"

Back onto the roof we went, back through the door I had kicked open, back down the dark stairs, and out through the lobby. We burst out into the street and ran—or, in my case, hobbled quickly—past a half-dozen men, shouting drunkenly, coming out of the tavern. As we reached the corner I glanced back and saw Sloan emerge from the alley leading behind his flophouse. He shouted something and shook his fist, and I waved at him before grabbing Meta's hand and plunging into the darkness of a side street.

Every step hurt as we zigzagged from block to block, ignoring and ignored by the shadowy, ragged people we passed. Finally, I stopped beneath the flickering blue light of a tube station, panting in time with Meta and contrapuntally to the assorted throbbings in my body. "Should be—safe enough," I gasped out. "Sloan—not one for running."

"I thought you were dead back there!"

"So did I. But no harm done..." To prove it, I ran my hands over my chest—and swore.

"What is it?"

"My pocket is empty!" I checked it again to be sure.

"So?"

"That's where I put my credchip. It must have fallen out when I went over the railing."

"You said you couldn't use it without Qualls or the 'forcers finding out where you are, anyway."

"Yeah, but in an emergency..." I sighed. "Well, better Andy Nebula's fortune falls three stories than Andy Nebula."

"You're not Andy Nebula anymore," Meta said flatly. I wondered how she felt about that. She looked up and down the empty street. "Now where?"

"Spaceport. We still have to get off this planet, and now—" I patted my pocket. "We have no choice. We have to stow away."

I led her to the port along deserted back streets. As we trudged along, Meta kept her head down. Finally she said, "Kit..."

"Yeah? Here, let's go this way." We turned down a narrow, dank alley. Overhead, first light greyed the clouds.

Meta halted. "Stop for a minute."

"Time's economic, gladeye."

"I said *stop!*"

I stopped.

Meta looked at me. "Are you *really* all right?"

"Of course I'm all right. The slug never touched me, thanks to my poor old stringsynth."

"I'm not talking about the slug."

I was silent for a moment. "I said awful things, didn't I?"

She didn't reply.

"That wasn't me, it was the flash."

Still nothing.

"You do understand that, don't you?"

"I—I guess so." She folded her arms over her chest, hugging herself. "But...you scared me. And even before Sloan's, you'd... one minute you'd be fine, and the next..."

"I know." I took her shoulders. "Meta, I swear, it was the flash. And it's over. I'm over it. I'm my old self again."

She looked down. "Your old self wasn't always nice, either."

"I didn't want to get you involved, that's all." But that wasn't all. I just hadn't wanted to be bothered. I'd been so wrapped up in my plans for my career that she'd been a nuisance I'd just wanted to be rid of. But then, when I'd needed her, I hadn't hesitated to involve her—in the worst possible way. She could have been the one the slug hit, back there on the roof, or...

Or, under the influence of flash, I could have killed her.

I let go of her. "Meta, I'm sorry for getting you into this—"

"I got myself into it." She raised her eyes. "Andy Nebula doesn't really exist. None of the Sensations Singles are what we're told they are. It's all a big lie."

What could I say? That's exactly what it was. "It's just—show business. You're not supposed to take it seriously."

"Not supposed to be as stupid as I was, you mean."

"That's not—"

"Oh, it's all right. My parents always told me I was wasting my time 'listening to that trash.' They kept telling me to grow up." She ran her fingers through her hair. "I guess I am. But I don't like it much."

"I'm sorry," I said again. I couldn't think of anything else.

"Yeah, well." She smiled, just a little. "I wanted to tell Bekka all about my adventures with Andy Nebula. I guess I won't have to make them up, after all." Her smile went away. "But tell me again. One more time. The absolute truth. *Are you really all right?*"

"Yes," I said, but I wondered. Deep down inside me, there was still a strange feeling, a not-quite itch, that made me wonder what would happen the *next* time someone offered me flash. I hoped I'd never find out. "We'd better hurry. We'll want to get to the spaceport before full light."

Ten minutes later, we stood crammed together in a dark doorway across the street from the terminal, looking for any sign of the Ice Boys. Nothing moved.

Of course, they could be hiding and watching like us. That street looked awfully wide and empty. But we had to cross it.

I straightened. "Look nonchalant," I said, but as we walked into the open, I felt as conspicuous as if I were naked and painted fluorescent green. Still, no shouts—or shots—echoed through the pre-dawn twilight and no mirrorcloth-clad killers came swarming after us: we crossed in perfect safety.

Was that because they were waiting for us inside?

No. The interior of the terminal was almost as deserted as the street had been, except for a few passengers waiting for some early lift-off and a handful of bored personnel yawning behind ticket counters. "It's too easy," I muttered.

"Maybe Qualls still thinks Sloan has you," Meta said.

That made sense. If he thought I'd already been captured, he had no need to set a new trap. And Sloan wouldn't tell him he'd lost us until he was sure he couldn't get us back. It surprised me he'd actually shot me. *I'll bet it was an accident, and he scared himself. That's why he ran down to the street instead of coming to look over the wall. If he'd killed me, he'd have had to get rid of my body before Qualls found out.*

"Well, then," I said, "all we have to worry about is sneaking on board a spaceship." I looked at Meta. "You're the expert there..."

"Easy. First you find your favourite singer's dressing room..."

I grinned. "Right idea. But instead of a dressing room, we look for a cargo module."

On a Pleasure Planet, security would have stopped us or shot us half a dozen times in the next few minutes, but I guess nobody on Murdoch IV thought any cargo arriving or departing from Fistfight City could possibly be worth interfering with. We simply found an unstaffed ticket counter, a long way from the nearest staffed one—plenty of those at that hour. Of course, the door behind it into the cargo area was locked, but there was a conveyor belt, currently stationary, that ordinarily took luggage from the counter back through the wall, and the only thing sealing it was a veil of flickering blue light. "Automated explosives, drugs, and weapons scan," I whispered to Meta as we crawled through the twinkling beams, feeling nothing. "It couldn't care less about stow-aways." *Probably not a good idea to crawl through it very often, given the radiation exposure*, I thought, but I didn't see any need to mention that.

We emerged into semi-darkness in another room. The conveyor belt continued through the back wall, next to a closed door. The room was otherwise empty except for a few coveralls and hardhats hung on hooks along the back wall. "Perfect," I said. I took what looked like the smallest pair of coveralls down and passed it to Meta. "Pull this on over your clothes."

I did the same, and then handed her a hardhat and took one for myself. Thus disguised—although Meta's coverall was so big on her she had to roll up the pant cuffs and sleeves, which made her look like a kid playing dress-up (which I guess, in a way, she was)—we went out into the large open space we had dodged through while escaping the Ice Boys.

Loud clangs and crashes from our right indicated some kind of work in progress. This time, we turned that direction and headed deeper into the building's entrails. We picked our way, banging shins every other step, it felt like, through a spider's nightmare of conveyor belts, platforms, and elevators, finally reaching the entrance of a huge chamber from which spilled the noise and (at last!) enough light to show us where we were putting our feet. Of course, it also showed us the chamber's metal gate and armed guards, and beyond them, more guards inspecting crates and boxes on one of the conveyor belts. Maybe

Murdochians weren't quite as trusting as I'd thought. "Now what?" Meta demanded.

I studied the situation for a minute, then a few minutes more. Meta fidgeted and once muttered something under her breath that I chose to ignore. "All right," I said. "Here's what we're going to do..."

Ten minutes later, I strode confidently (with only a slight limp) up to the gate. I grinned at the guards. "Hi, guys," I said, started past them—and felt a meaty hand on my arm.

"Where's your security badge, kid?"

"Huh? It's right—" I put my hand on the left side of my chest, glanced down, and swore. "It must have fallen off back in the locker room. I'll be right back—" I turned to go, and suddenly the conveyor belt on which the crates were being inspected whirred to life. The inspectors shouted and lunged at the crates, but too late to stop the one farthest along from crashing off the end of the belt, spilling glittery bits of something shiny and fragile across the duracrete floor.

The guards and I dashed over to rescue the remaining crates before they joined the first. A wild-eyed woman kept frantically slapping at the controls. I could have told her that was a waste of time, because I'd jammed the controls at the other end of the belt. When we finally got all the crates off the belt and onto the floor, the control-slapping woman led the other inspectors in a heated argument with the guards over whose fault it all was.

"Well, gotta get to work," I said cheerfully, and walked calmly into the loading area. Once out of sight, I stopped and looked around. "Meta?" I called cautiously.

"Here!" She emerged, somewhat breathless, from between two crates. "I can't believe it worked."

"Of course it worked. My ideas always work." I ignored her withering look. "Come on, let's see where we are."

The crashing and banging we'd been hearing came from a single forklift, moving hexagonal containers into a larger orange container—a cargo module. Just what we were looking for, although that particular one wouldn't do, since it was packed solid. The one we were standing next to, though...

I hurried down to the far end of it and peered cautiously around the corner. No one in sight, which made me happy. What made me even happier was the pressure door in the middle of the short end of the module, with a protruding keypad to the left of it and a glowing control panel next to that. I hurried over and took a good look. "Perfect!"

Meta came up behind me. "What is?"

I pointed at the control panel. "Life-support controls. This is a pressurized cargo module. Whatever they're shipping in it doesn't like vacuum, and since I don't, either..."

"But how do we get in?"

"We don't, if it's locked. But if it's not fully loaded yet..."

I touched the button on the keypad helpfully labeled OPEN, and the door swung inward. Blue lights came on inside.

I waved Meta in. "After you."

17

CREEPY SHIPMATES

It shouldn't have been that easy.

It wasn't.

Inside, the module—which was much smaller than my dressing room, really just the kind of container you'd see on the back of a ground transport vehicle—consisted of a long, narrow aisle between tall shelves that ran the length of the module. The metal shelves—five on each side, about a metre and a half deep with maybe fifty or sixty centimetres between each shelf and the one above, with the bottom shelf right at floor level—were empty.

"No place to hide," said Meta as the door closed behind us. "Maybe this module isn't going with the others."

"Maybe," I said. "But then, why activate it? It takes energy to power it, and energy is money. I think we're just early."

"But the first person who opens the door—"

As if on cue, the door opened. I froze and waited to be caught—but no one came in. I could hear voices just around the corner, though, male and indistinct. "All the way to the end," I whispered to Meta. "Quick!"

"But there's nothing—"

"Move!" She moved. The module ended in a bulkhead. "Bottom shelves," I said, and replied to her puzzled look by lying down on the floor, squeezing onto the lowermost shelf, and then pushing myself hard against the wall. I turned my head in time to see Meta wriggling with less difficulty onto the bottom shelf on the other side.

Seconds later, a pair of steel-toed work boots clumped into sight. A second pair of boots followed.

"Lots of room," said a voice. "We won't use half of it."

"Good," growled a second, deeper voice. "The fewer of these things I have to carry, the better."

"You got that right. Ugliest critters I ever set my eyes on."

"Looked in a mirror recently, Pete?"

"Shut up, Dargo." They went out, but I met Meta's frightened eyes and shook my head, warning her to stay quiet and stay still.

The boots came back. "So, what do you suppose they use them for?" said Pete.

"I don't know. Food, maybe."

"That's disgusting!"

"Have you looked in a—"

"Oh, suck vacuum." Out and back again; more banging noises over our heads. "Maybe they're pets."

"Shut up and load." After that they stayed silent, except for the occasional grunt, as they moved in and out, gradually working their way toward the door. I fought an overwhelming urge to sneeze and wondered what we were bunking with.

At last they finished. I heard the door close, but the lights stayed on. As quickly as I could—not very—I wormed out from under the shelf. Meta was quicker; she stood up and screamed.

"Stop that!" I said irritably. Then I stood up and almost screamed, too.

Locked into magnetic holders every half-metre along the middle shelves were glass-walled crates holding...well, monsters: eight-legged reptilian creatures with scaly, whiplike tails and four glittering golden eyes apiece on stalks atop long, narrow heads. Every eye locked on us when we moved—and every mouth opened, revealing long black fangs and gums the colour of a dead man's face.

And then the lights went out.

"Kit..." said Meta, voice quavering. "I'm going to scre—eee!"

"That's me, that's me," I said, squeezing her arm.

"What *are* they?"

"Food—pets—I don't know. You heard as much as I did."

"Nobody could eat *those*." I felt her shudder.

"Well, they can't get out. They're nothing to worry about."

"Why did the lights go out? What's happening?"

"I think they must be getting ready to load this module. We've almost made it!"

"So what do we do?"

"Sit. Wait."

"For what?"

"Lift-off." I eased myself down onto the floor, and leaned back against the bulkhead. "Remember what I told you aboard *The Bullet*. Once we're in space, it's too expensive to return. Whatever happens, wherever we end up, at least we'll be away from Fistfight City—and Qualls."

I heard Meta sit beside me; I reached out for her and she flinched, then grabbed my hand and squeezed—hard. "That's a little—ouch!—tight," I said.

"Sorry." Meta loosened her grip. "It's just—I keep imagining those—those things getting out, and—" She shuddered again. "I hate snakes and things like that."

"I hate snakes and things like that, too," I said grimly. "And the biggest snake I know is Qualls."

Meta moved closer; I could feel her warmth. "Kit—"

"What?" I closed my eyes; it made the unrelenting blackness easier to bear.

"Will you—will you hold me?"

My eyes flew open. "Uh—"

"I don't mean, like *that,* I just... " Her voice trailed off. "I just want to be sure you're there."

I put my arms around her and pulled her close. "Of course I'm here."

She snuggled against me, her head on my chest. "Thank you," she whispered.

After that, we sat in the silent darkness, waiting for whatever would happen next.

Not surprisingly, what happened next was we both fell asleep.

I surfaced slowly, like a man trying to swim in thick mud, from a disturbed dream involving running, fire, and giant rats. I struggled to wakefulness and finally jerked upright with a gasp, waking Meta. "What's wrong?" she cried.

"Bad dream, that's all." I wiped cold sweat from my forehead. "Go back to sleep."

Good advice—but I knew I couldn't take it. That dream had

come from flash. I *knew* it. I had broken the physical addiction—hadn't I?—but the mental effects—would I ever be free of them? And if *one dose* could do this to me, what would have been left of me after two years on Hydra and a constant diet of the stuff?

Two years? In a time pocket, it would be more like thirty.

I thought of Paris Paradise and all the other kids Qualls had passed on to The Dealer, and clenched my fists. He had a lot to answer for. A *lot*.

A bass rumble shook the floor. "Meta?" I whispered.

"What?" Her hand tightened in the folds of my shirt.

"They've activated the lifters. We've done it!"

"Does that mean we can get out of here soon?"

I laughed and hugged her. "Soon," I said. "Very soon."

The rumble rose in pitch and volume. I had a fleeting feeling of extra weight before the gravsims overrode the acceleration—but then I frowned. Now I was *too* light. "Must be a freighter," I muttered. "Their gravsims are out of whack. It can't be a regular passenger ship."

I wished I'd thought to see what ships were in port. Maybe I could have figured out which one we were on—and where we were going. I thought about the creatures surrounding us in the dark (then kind of wished I hadn't). What world would want something like that? I had no idea.

I gave the ship half an hour to break orbit, to ensure the captain would have no inclination to return to Fistfight City. Then I woke Meta, who had dozed off again, and climbed stiffly to my feet. "We must have slept for hours," I groaned, trying to work the kinks out of my back and legs. I stretched, accidentally touched the cold smooth surface of one of the animal containers, and snatched my hand back as though burned.

Glad I'd been invisible to Meta in the dark, I felt my way down the module toward the door. There had to be some way to open it from the inside...I fumbled around until I felt a protruding keypad like the one on the other side of the door. I poked at it blindly, something clicked sharply, and the module's interior lights came on. I blinked. Blue and harsh, they made me want to squint, at least I could see. "That's better," I murmured, and pushed the OPEN button. The door, to the right of the keypad, swung inward—the hinges were on the far side. To my surprise, we weren't in a dark hold, but hooked up to a corridor, filled with the same weird blue light as the module—only brighter.

Meta winced. "That hurts!"

"Must be a real rustbucket," I said. "Weak gravsims and bad lighting. I hope it holds together long enough to get us wherever we're going."

I stepped out of the module and looked both ways. To the left, the corridor ran about a dozen metres, ending in another door. To the right, it ended in a T-intersection. "Well, let's go face the music," I told Meta, and strode down the corridor—no need to hide now that we *wanted* to be found—stepped into the intersection, looked left—and leaped back, crashing into Meta.

She opened her mouth, but I clapped my hand over it to keep her quiet and pushed her away from the corner. She stared at me wide-eyed. I signalled *Shhh!* with a finger on my lips, then released her mouth, took her arm, and almost dragged her back to "our" module. The moment we were inside, I slapped the button that closed the door behind us, then released her and fell back against it.

Meta stared at me. "Kit, what's wrong?"

My knees gave out. Watched eagerly by monsters, I sank to the floor, my back to the closed door that suddenly seemed like no protection at all.

"The Dealer," I whispered. "We're on The Dealer's ship!"

THE TIME POCKET

META TURNED white and slid down beside me. "It can't be!"

"I saw him—right out there!" I jerked my thumb over my shoulder.

"Are you sure?"

"I'd recognize him anywhere."

"But how can this be *his* ship? *Nobody* owns his own ship!"

That stopped me, because it was true: no individual was that wealthy. Only large corporations or governments could afford to run ships. And if The Dealer *had* had his own ship, why would he have been a passenger on the *The Bullet*—and why was *The Bullet* supposed to have taken me to Hydra?

"You're right," I said. "This must be a Hydran passenger liner! Without me, Qualls's contract with The Dealer fell through, so Qualls wouldn't have any reason to go to Hydra— but The Dealer still had to get home. So he had to buy a ticket just like anyone else." Which meant all we had to do was avoid The Dealer and find a crewhydra.

But if this was a passenger ship, why was The Dealer in the cargo section? The answer seemed obvious—he had cargo down here he wanted to keep an eye on. I looked nervously at the caged beasts surrounding us, but if he'd been headed to our module when I saw him, he would have already found us. So he must have gone somewhere else.

With the help of the shelving, I got to my feet, then reached out a hand to pull Meta to hers. "Come on. Let's take another look."

"If you say so..." she said dubiously.

I opened the door, led her out into the corridor again, crept up to the T-intersection, and very cautiously looked both ways—no sign of The Dealer. I rounded the corner and started toward the place where I had seen him. Meta grabbed my arm to stop me. "Shouldn't we go the *other* way?" she whispered.

"No," I whispered back. "I want to see what his cargo is."

"But what if he's still there..."

"We'll be careful."

She sighed and followed me down to the spot where The Dealer had stood. He'd been outside the doorway to another module, identical to the entrance to ours, right down to the green indicators on the life-support control panel.

What could The Dealer be shipping that required life support?

Suddenly, I thought I knew. I swore and reached for the keypad.

Meta grabbed my wrist. "What are you doing?"

"Opening this thing up," I snarled.

"But why—"

"Life-support module. There's something alive in there." I met her eyes. "Besides flash, what does The Dealer deal in?"

Meta's hand fell away. "No!"

"I hope I'm wrong. Maybe he's got a cat. But we've got to be sure—dammit!" Of course, the OPEN button didn't work—the module was locked. I pointed to a black slot on the top of the keypad. "We need either an access code or a keychip—neither of which we have." I glared at the controls. "There's got to be a way!"

"Well, I've got a keychip," Meta said, "but since it's for our house back on Carstair's Folly, I doubt—"

A wild idea struck me. "Let me have it!"

Looking at me like I'd lost my mind, Meta pulled a neck-chain from under her blouse. Hanging from it was a little golden rectangle with flat-black contact patches on one end. Meta touched it, and it dropped off into her hand. She handed it to me. I held it up next to the slot on top of the keypad. "Standard technology. Come on!"

I dashed back down the corridor to our module. Filled with monsters though it was, it seemed almost like home. Meta's keychip fit neatly into a slot on top of the inner keypad. I pushed three buttons, the controls beeped, and the keychip popped out again. I grabbed it.

"What did you do?" Meta asked.

"Programmed your keychip to open *this* module." I gestured at the animals. "I don't know what these things are, but I'll bet they belong to The Dealer. They look like friends of his, don't they?"

Meta blinked, then grinned. "I get it! If this module belongs to him, and we now have a keychip for it—"

"Then just maybe we have a keychip for that other module, too." I flipped the chip like a coin. "Only one way to find out."

Back we went to the other module. I plugged the keychip into the receptacle, pressed the "open" button—and without any fuss at all, the door slid aside.

Normal white light spilled around us. It was a relief to step out of the blue Hydran glare—until I saw what was in there.

The module was about the same size and shape as my old dressing room, several times bigger than the one we'd stowed away in. Odd-looking bits of electronic equipment filled most of, giving it the look of a cross between a starship bridge and a recording studio, the latter resemblance heightened by the boy, my age or a little older, who stood in a broad circle of light at the far end of the module. He wore gold tights, but was naked from the waist up.

"Hello!" said Meta cheerfully, and started forward, but I stopped her. "Now what?" she demanded, turning on me.

"He's not breathing."

"What?" She turned back toward the boy. "Of course he's—" Her voice broke off.

"See?"

"But that's—impossible."

"Is it?" I moved gingerly forward. Meta followed. The closer we got to the boy the more I became aware of an annoying hum, a discordant sound that grated on my nerves. The air within the circle of light around the boy sparkled strangely.

We stopped just outside that circle. The hum made my bones itch. Meta gasped. "I know that face! That's Paul Jerez!"

"Who?"

"He was Youth Champion in the Pleasure Planets' Annual

Open Dance Competition last year—then he vanished. There were all kinds of wild rumours..." She came a little closer. "It must be a statue—or maybe a waxwork."

I said nothing. No waxwork could be so detailed. I could see the fine, dark hair on his arms and chest and a few flyaway strands sticking up from his head. His eyes, open and moist, glistened in the light, his lips were slightly parted, and a single bead of sweat clung to his left temple—and yet he didn't breathe, didn't swallow, didn't blink. *Time pocket,* I thought. Almost involuntarily, I reached out to touch him. The sparkling circle of light retreated—

—and suddenly snapped back out to its original position, engulfing my hand and stopping me cold. I couldn't move my hand: couldn't raise it, lower it, push it forward, twitch my fingers, clench my fist, or—most frightening of all—pull it free.

"What—" Meta started forward.

I pushed her back with my left arm. "Stay away! I'm stuck."

"Stuck? On what?"

I didn't answer. I was too busy silently cursing myself for a fool. I'd known it was a time pocket, and I'd still stuck my hand into it.

Inside that pocket, time did not pass, or passed very slowly, for Paul—and now, for my hand. That momentary shrinking of the field, which I'd stupidly ignored, had probably been a safety feature—or maybe, knowing The Dealer, a trap: a trap that had caught me like a bug in amber.

Sweat formed on my forehead. I couldn't feel my hand at all —it might have been lopped off. But I could see it, the air sparkling around it—and I could see the beat of my pulse in my wrist outside that sparkle, and I could certainly feel the pressure in my arm as my heart and arteries tried futilely to push blood into my hand, a throbbing building toward pain.

"Go get help," I gasped to Meta. "Someone in the crew."

"But you—"

"I'll be fine—if you hurry. Take the keychip and go!"

Meta hesitated a moment longer, then dashed out into the corridor, turning to look back at me as she snatched the keychip out of the control panel. The door slid closed.

I pulled at my hand as hard as I could, to no effect, then heard the door open again behind me and breathed a sigh of relief. *That was quick!* "Meta, I—"

My voice choked off as I turned my head to look awkwardly over my shoulder.

"Mr. Nebula," said The Dealer, "I see you have decided to fulfill your contract after all."

19

BETRAYAL

"SUCK VACUUM, SNAKEBRAIN," I snarled.

"Mr. Nebula!" The Dealer entered, the door closing behind him. "Surely it is not appropriate, even among humans, to talk that way to one's employer. Or the one individual on this ship who can provide—this." He wore a belt like his hench-hydras had back in Fistfight City, with several things hanging from it. One of those was a silver cylinder. He touched it. When he raised that tentacle again, a green wafer rested on one of his finger-tentacles, glowing in the light against his orange skin

My body's immediate reaction shocked me—my heart raced, my mouth filled with saliva, I shivered. *I beat you!* I wanted to yell. *I don't need you anymore!* Maybe so—but I wanted it. Not so much I couldn't fight it—maybe—but I wanted it.

I tried not to show it. "No joy, octoface. I beat the green monster."

The Dealer moved closer, all four eyes fixed on me though their stalks curled and twisted, until he held the flash within centimetres of my mouth. "And you suffered for it, didn't you?" his strange, sexless voice crooned. "Suffered and almost died. But you still want it, don't you?" The flash was so close I could have stuck out my tongue and taken it, and I found myself gaping like a fish out of water, mouth opening and closing. But I held on. Focusing fiercely on the pounding pain in my arm, I turned my head away.

Then I suggested The Dealer do something to himself for which he wasn't physically equipped. He imitated human laughter. "Very brave. But stupid. You're mine, Andy Nebula. I have a signed contract for your services."

"But you've never paid for me!"

"It's hardly my fault you chose to—what's the human expression?—ah, yes, 'cut your agent out of the deal.'"

"It's enough to break that contract!"

"You're in no position to take me to court." Two of The Dealer's eyes turned toward Paul. "Any more than he is."

Agony filled my arm now. I pulled helplessly at my hand.

"Experiencing a little discomfort?" queried The Dealer.

"Damn you—"

He laughed again and scuttled over to the controls. The circle of sparkling air shrank by a few centimetres, freeing my hand. Immediately the pain in my arm subsided and my hand flushed red and felt hot; but, oddly, it didn't tingle. I suppose, from its point of view, it had never been deprived of blood at all. I flexed the fingers; no damage. Then I turned to look at The Dealer. "What about Paul?"

"He is doing quite well where he is."

The door slid open. My heart leaped at the sight of Meta and a hydra—and then fell when the hydra, far from rushing to my rescue, shoved Meta to the floor, then closed the door. I recognized him now as the giant hydra who had pinned me in my dressing room in Fistfight City. He squealed/clicked at The Dealer, who pulled Meta roughly to her feet and held her off the floor while three of his eyes focused on her face. The fourth stayed firmly aimed at me. "That was very foolish of you, young lady. And futile. This ship is crewed by robots and captained by a computer. We have never shared the human phobia against putting ourselves in the tentacles of well-made machines. And while those machines are programmed to stop one hydra from hurting another, they're not programmed to recognize humans at all." His tentacles tightened around Meta, who gasped. Her legs kicked futilely.

I lunged toward The Dealer, but the big hydra moved with blinding speed to grab me. The Dealer held Meta a moment longer, then dropped her. "Interesting," he said, as she frantically crawled away from him on her hands and knees. "A protective impulse toward the female. No doubt another evolutionary byproduct of your absurd binary method of reproduction."

"Are you all right?" I called to Meta.

"Yes," she said. "I'm sorry, Kit, I looked everywhere but—"

A robot ship...if The Dealer was telling the truth, and I had a sinking feeling he was, we were in deep, deep biowaste.

Or at least I was. "So you've got me," I said. "Let Meta go."

"Go where?" said The Dealer. "There is nowhere to go until we reach my homeworld."

"Then let her go when we get there! She's no use to you. She's only here because..." *Because I was a selfish fool and asked her to help me.* "...because of me."

"But once we reach Hydra," said The Dealer, "she might tell

someone about my operation, the wrong someone." He turned toward Meta, and the green wafer appeared on his tentacle again. "Fortunately, I can ensure she doesn't."

"*No!*" I screamed, and struggled to reach him, but the tentacles of the big hydra held me like steel bands.

Meta, eyes wide, backed away from The Dealer, who stalked her, his human laughter fading into a hail of clicks. He lashed out and I flinched, but she ducked, then scrambled to the door and slapped at the control panel. The Dealer shot after her, but she threw herself through the doorway before it was open enough for The Dealer to follow. When he could, she was gone.

"Orbital, Meta!" I yelled after her, although her name ended in a squeak as the big hydra holding me tightened his grip.

The Dealer turned back. "Let her roam the ship. She can do us no harm, and there's no place for her to hide." He closed the door, then stood stock still for a moment before his eyes swung back to look at me. "Or is there? How did you stow away?"

"Sneaked on during loading," I said, hoping Meta had been smart enough to head back to the monster cage—and that she'd be brave enough to return with the keychip later and try another rescue. The Dealer and his friend couldn't stay in here forever. "It wasn't hard." I shrugged. "Now I know why. No crew."

The Dealer squealed and the big hydra let me go. "Then how did you get into this module?"

"I've been fragging locks since half-height, octoman," I sneered. "Good programming for those mean old streets, pre-Qualls." Time to get *off* this subject. "Where is Qualls, anyway?"

"No doubt striving very hard to find the money to buy his

way out of his contract with me," said The Dealer. "Since he let you escape, he owes me my expected revenue from your services. The penalty for defaulting is rather severe."

"You wouldn't dare take him to court."

"I wasn't speaking of a *legal* penalty."

Oh. "But you've got me, now."

The Dealer lifted, then dropped, his tentacles—a Hydran shrug? "And so I double my revenue. An excellent deal, don't you think?"

The big hydra shrieked, and The Dealer shrieked back. Without warning, the big hydra slapped a sticky gag across my mouth and shoved me into the corner. Before I could recover my balance, he picked up a fat white tube and pointed it at me. A sticky green web engulfed me, pinning my legs together and my arms to my torso. I teetered and crashed to the floor. The big hydra propped me up in the corner like a rag doll, then scuttled back.

The Dealer stared down at me with all four eyes. "I'm low on flash. I see no reason to waste it on you," he said. "You're fortunate; now you will get to see for yourself what I have planned for you, and why you are valuable." He squealed and the door opened again, revealing a new hydra. As it and The Dealer exchanged ear-piercing greetings, my eyes widened.

Rain!

I felt sick. The message in Fistfight City *had* been a trap! Rain must have hoped to capture me and sell me back to The Dealer.

He was in on the whole deal. My meeting him in Fat Sloan's on that months-ago rainy night had been no accident. Rain had played his part well, cleverly manoeuvring me to the spaceport the next day, right into Qualls's clutches...

I tried to kick, to bang my head, to do something to attract his attention so he could see my hate-filled glare, but the webbing held, and Rain had eyes only for The Dealer and for Paul Jerez, still motionless in his circle of light.

The Dealer held out the green wafer he had tempted me with, and two others. Rain took them, but didn't eat them. Instead he held them while The Dealer returned to his controls.

The circle of light expanded, elongating into an oval that almost touched my feet. The itching filled my bones again—then eased. And then Paul moved, turning expectantly in the oval, his eyes raised but unfocused, as though he were looking at something farther away than the walls of the module. The Dealer clicked to Rain, who stepped inside the circle with none of the difficulty I had experienced—and then, to my horror, held out one of the green wafers to Paul, who took it gently from the end of one orange tentacle with his pink tongue, and swallowed.

As Rain watched, music began. Paul paused, moved, made a heartbreakingly graceful spin—and then The Dealer touched his controls and the circle flashed with light, and instantly Paul was standing three metres away from where he had started, his bare chest heaving and streaked with sweat. He bowed to Rain, who squealed and clicked enthusiastically. As I gaped at them, Paul returned to centre stage, Rain held out another wafer, Paul took it—and then Rain took one himself.

The music began again, Paul made the same—*exactly* the same—magnificent leap and spin, The Dealer touched his controls, the circle flashed, and there was Paul, again at the end of his dance, glistening with sweat, bowing to Rain.

Paul returned to the middle of the circle and assumed his ready-and-waiting, Rain stepped out of the circle, The Dealer did something at the controls, the circle shrank—and Paul froze, in the middle of a deep breath, his chest suddenly stilled.

I stared at him, horrified. No wonder Paris Paradise had aged so quickly. No wonder he had gone crazy. How many years of performing the same number—*exactly* the same number—before hallucinatory crowds had The Dealer crammed into Paris's two-year contract? He could have done the same song a thousand times while only minutes passed in the outside world.

And Qualls had sold me and my predecessors into *that*? Subjective years of drug-induced slavery, performing a dreary Sensation Single thousands of times for equally drug-crazed hydras? If I could have made a sound, I would have screamed my rage. But helpless as luggage, I could only lie there and pray that somehow I could find a way out of this. Because if I didn't, I would soon be as old and crazy as Paris Paradise.

Rain left without ever turning an eye in my direction; The Dealer and the other hydra followed him to the door. The big hydra squealed a question, but The Dealer, obviously using Fedspeech for my benefit, said, "Leave him. He's not going anywhere and without his help the girl can never break in here. It will do him good to think over what he's seen. Welcome to your new life, Mr. Nebula!" he called to me; then, with an eerie mixture of human and hydra laughter, he went out, and the door closed behind him.

20

FANGS

I MIGHT HAVE GIVEN up hope then, except I knew The Dealer was wrong. Meta *could* get back in. She still had the keychip.

I wriggled around until I had a clear view of the door, and waited for it to open. Any minute now, she'd come in and free me, and then—there had to be some way to get help, some kind of emergency communicator, or some way to talk to the computer, or—

But Meta didn't come back, and didn't come back, and didn't come back, while my legs and arms tingled, then grew numb. I wriggled, trying to force blood into my limbs, but the hydra's tanglegun had netted me too tightly. If Meta didn't come soon, I might not even be able to walk.

She didn't come soon. *They've found her,* I thought bitterly. The Dealer would show up soon, addict her to flash to ensure her cooperation, and then use her as a hostage to ensure mine.

And the scary thing was, I knew it would work.

Back in Fistfight City I'd avoided making "friends." The kind of friends you made on the street were worse than a nuisance. They died, or disappeared, or cheated or robbed you the first chance they got. I'd taken care of myself and liked it that way. Back then, I wouldn't have lifted a finger to save a rich kid like Meta, or anyone else. Other people weren't my concern. I had my own problems.

But Meta...Meta really was a friend, the first real friend I'd ever had. She'd already rescued me once. If The Dealer had her, I would do anything to free her—even sign a legal contract.

That's it! I thought suddenly. *If he has me legally, it won't matter what she tells anyone. He'll let her go!*

And I'd be like poor Paris Paradise, like the frozen figure of Paul Jerez, still streaked with sweat from a dance that he'd performed hours ago in real time, drugged, hypnotized, locked in a bubble of alternity.

Better that than Meta addicted to flash, or simply murdered.

The adrenalin of being captured drained away, the fear of what would happen next and the expectation of Meta's entrance followed, and in their absence, my body took a notion to do the natural thing—sleep.

I woke in terror and thrashed around wildly, coming out of a horrible dream where I was surrounded by hydras trying to stuff gigantic wafers of flash into my mouth—and rolled right into Meta, who squeaked and fell over. I blinked at her over my gag as she crawled back to me and went to work on my bonds with my knife. "Mmmmph. Mmmmmmmmmmph!" I demanded, and she pulled off my gag, taking what little facial hair I had with it. "Took you long enough," I grumbled.

"That big hydra was outside for hours. He finally went away

—had to go to the bathroom or something, I guess." She stopped clipping for a second. "How *do* hydras go to the bathroom?"

"If you don't hurry you'll be able to ask The Dealer himself!"

She redoubled her efforts, but the sticky green web from the big hydra's tanglegun didn't yield easily. It took several minutes to free me and it was several more before I could stand, on legs that burned and tingled. I swayed. "Can you walk?" Meta asked anxiously.

"If I can't, I'll crawl. Let's get out of here."

I almost did have to crawl. My legs didn't want to work, and twice I stumbled on the way to the door. I hesitated there for a minute. Should I wait for my legs to recover? If the big hydra was back, we'd have to run for it—

But then I remembered just how fast that hydra could move. If we had to run, we were already caught. Our only hope was that the hydra had been called away by something more than nature—or else that hydras took a long time to go to the bathroom.

I opened the door onto a deserted corridor. Glad we hadn't waited, I led the way back toward our monster-filled module. As we reached the corner, a bloodcurdling screech exploded behind us. I took one look back, saw the big hydra racing toward us, tentacles lashing, and grabbed Meta's hand and dragged her the rest the way, yelling at her to have the keychip ready. She slapped it in place, snatched it out again as the door opened, and we tumbled inside, then both turned and almost collided trying to get the door closed again before—

A red-orange tentacle the size of a freighter's fuel hose lashed through the closing door, grabbed my ankle, and yanked.

Pain exploded in the back of my head as my skull cracked against the metal floor. I slammed my other foot against the door to keep from being pulled out. The door, sensing the tentacle, stopped, beeped a warning, and started to slide open again. "Meta!" I screamed, and she hit the CLOSE control again. The door tried to close, failed, started to open. While Meta played cat and mouse with it, I struggled frantically against the hydra's pull. How much strength did those tentacles have? I had a gruesome vision of my leg tearing off, and then screamed as my boot ripped painfully off my foot, the tentacle vanished, and the door closed and locked at last.

One foot bare, I staggered up, ignoring the goggling, golden eyes of the creatures in the cages. Better those monsters than the one in the hallway. "We've got to disable that door," I gasped out. "We've got to lock ourselves in!"

Meta stared at me, then at the shelves of monsters. "In *here*?"

"The Dealer has a keychip for this!" My leg had hurt before—now I could hardly move it. I pulled myself up to the door controls. "If we can reprogram the lock, or break it—"

A light on the panel flashed green. "Back!" I screamed, and retreated, staggering, pushing Meta to the end of the module, as the door opened.

It framed the big hydra—who stepped aside to reveal The Dealer. "You're more resourceful than I thought, Mr. Nebula," he said, skittering into the module on his crablike legs, and something about the way he said it, even in that neuter Hydran voice, made my skin crawl. Or maybe it was the way all four eyes glared at me, and the ends of his tentacles curled and uncurled. "But I simply can't waste any more time with you, or your annoying female friend. Too much more disturbance and the captain-computer may take some unwelcome notice."

One of his eyes scanned the cages. "It is curious you should have chosen this particular cargo module in which to stow away, Mr. Nebula. As you may recall, I mentioned I am low on flash, which was why I postponed your conditioning. However, it occurs to me that you might be the perfect subject for an experiment, since, to an extent, you are expendable—Qualls will, after all, pay me what you would be worth as a performer, so should the experiment fail, all I would lose would be the extra revenue I could have made from having both your services *and* his payment. I'm willing to risk that." A tentacle reached out and caressed the glass front of one of the cages. The creature inside followed the movement intently. "These beauties are called (hiss(click)screech). I don't believe they have a name in your language, yet."

"If these are your pets, snakehead, you must be hard up for friends," I snarled.

"Oh, they're hardly pets. They're quite poisonous. Spawnlings have nightmares about them. But, I confess, I'm attracted to them." His tentacle toyed with the lock on the cage. "You see, it is the venom of these creatures that we render into flash."

I shuddered. The Dealer continued to stroke the cage, as if hypnotized by the creature within—or as if trying to hypnotize *it*. "Of course, in the living creature the active substance is far more concentrated. I would imagine that one bite from the fangs of my little friend here would be the equivalent of a hundred or more normal human doses of flash. I know what that does to *us*—and it is, indeed, nightmare fuel—but no one, to my knowledge, has ever conducted the experiment to see what it does to humans." All his eyes swivelled to me. "I think it's time to do so."

"You won't let that thing out while you're standing next to it," I said. "You're bluffing."

"Mr. Nebula, I don't *have* to let it out while I'm standing next to it. This lock—" his tentacle played over it, to the accompaniment of faint beeping— "is now programmed to open by itself after a certain amount of time has elapsed. I won't tell you exactly how long; that would spoil the suspense for you. However, by the time I return, I'm sure I'll be able to observe the results of my little test." One eye flicked toward Meta. "On both of you."

He started to back out; I shouted, "Wait!"

The Dealer paused. "Yes?"

"Let Meta go. I'll sign a legal contract with you. I'll swear I joined up with you of my own free will!"

"Mr. Nebula, the legitimacy of your contract was of concern to Qualls; it is of no concern to me. My only concern is ensuring that you stop causing me trouble. Should the two of you survive this little test, I suspect you will never again be able to free yourself from flash dependency, which will make you much easier to control. Should you die, dissection and analysis of your tissues will provide me with information no other flashdealer has about the effects of flash on humans. It could lead to an improved, more potent form of the drug, over which I would have sole control. As they say on your planet, 'data's economic, gladeye.' Either way, I lose nothing." He turned three of his eyes to the door panel. "Now, I really must reprogram this—"

I don't know where the idea came from; I don't remember

having it. All I know is that as The Dealer looked away, I grabbed the cage closest to me, jerked it free, and flung it at him.

He ducked, shrieking rage, all four eyes snapping toward me—but when he ducked, the cage smashed into the lock panel, and three things happened: the door slid shut, locking the big hydra outside, the cage shattered into a million sparkling shards—and the monstrosity it contained dropped squarely into the middle of The Dealer's tentacles.

I clapped my hands over my ears as he squealed, a sound of pure horror escalating into the ultrasonic. He scrabbled frantically with his tentacles, all four eyes curving inward to stare down at the creature even as it bit deep into his flesh.

The Dealer's stalk stiffened, every tentacle snapped straight out—and then they drooped, all four eyes staring sightlessly downward. The Dealer's legs folded, his stalk dropped with a thump—and the creature that had bitten him scrambled down past his breathing slits and onto the floor.

The thing's golden eyes scanned the room, seemingly ignoring us—but then Meta shifted her position, ever-so-slightly, and the eyes snapped around and locked on us. Slowly, lifting and placing each leg deliberately, the horror stalked the length of the cargo module, its brethren in the other cages watching it hungrily.

My heart raced; Meta draw a long shuddering breath. Why didn't the big hydra come raging in to help The Dealer? I stared at the thing on the floor and thought I could make a pretty good guess.

It still wasn't sure we were prey. A couple of metres away, it stopped. I tried not to breathe, tried to ignore all the aches and pains clamouring for my attention, tried to think of myself as a rock, a piece of metal, anything inanimate and, above all, motionless. The thing took another step toward us, halted, then moved a little closer yet. I thought about Meta behind me, and wondered which one of us would scream first.

And then, suddenly, the creature made up its mind and scuttled forward. Meta shrieked and tried to climb the shelves, and the creature instantly altered course and dashed for her.

"No!" I yelled. I lunged for it, fell headlong in front of it, grabbed it—and echoed Meta's shriek as its dead-white mouth snapped open and its shining black fangs sank deep into my wrist.

2 1

FLASHDEVIL FINALE

FIRE RACED through my veins and exploded in my head, erasing reality. The cargo module disappeared, dissolving into a narrow backstage corridor lined with banks of video monitors. Music pounded in my ears and I held a stringsynth in my hand.

I rolled to my feet, clutching it tight. I'd worked for this moment all my life—millions would be watching on vid, tens of thousands awaited me just beyond that curtain at the end of the monitor-lined corridor, beyond that broken-down dancebot half-blocking the way. The pounding of the music surged louder in my ears. Time for my entrance—why was the curtain still down?

But then it opened, and I saw another dancebot, this one fully functional, between me and the stage. Exultantly, I dashed forward, leaped over the broken 'bot, and reached for the second, but it turned and ran away from me, out into the bright stage lights.

The crowd roared, but I was furious. A malfunctioning 'bot,

tonight of all nights? Marcel would hear about this! I dashed after it, stringsynth loose in my hand, but the 'bot kept moving away from me, staggering, obviously bugging out. The roar of the crowd turned to boos, and then to laughter—and in a rage I flung the stringsynth at the dancebot.

It struck the machine squarely in the head in a shower of sparks and smoke. The 'bot froze, then toppled with a grinding, ear-splitting shriek of tortured metal.

The music still pounded around me and the crowd was still watching. I had to give my fans a show! I raced forward, snatching up the stringsynth. Another dancebot appeared in front of me, as obstructive as the previous one. Had they all crashed at once?

My anger swelled again, and I reared back to throw the stringsynth, but something grabbed my arm from behind and shrieked in my ear. The sound rang my head like a bell, the echoes resolving slowly into words: "Kit, no!"

For a handful of seconds, the stage, the dancebots, and the music faded away, and I saw, as dimly as if it were a bad holo-projection, the corridor outside the cargo module. The big hydra stood in front of me like the Dealer had, inert, collapsed. Behind him cowered Rain. Meta had seized my arm, and in my hand I held, not a stringsynth, but, wriggling and hissing, the horrible creature that had bitten me.

Rain! Meta didn't know he was in league with the Dealer! I struggled to pull free of her grasp, to throw the monster at Rain as I'd started to, but it shifted in my hand and lunged instead at Meta, and in horror I broke loose and threw it against the wall with all my strength. It hit with a horrible wet, crunching sound and slid to the floor, leaving behind a green, glistening streak.

But I couldn't hold onto reality against the river of venom racing through my veins. The corridor blew away like smoke in a hurricane, returning me to the dark stage and the pounding music. I dashed forward, shouldering past the dancebot I no longer remembered as Rain, and burst onto a huge stage. Light exploded around me and I screamed as flaming daggers lanced into my head, through my eyes, my ears, my nose, my mouth. Acid poured onto my body, eating away my skin, stripping me down to the bone, driving me to my knees. Still screaming, I staggered back to my feet and careened stage right, trying to outrun the agony.

I left the stage behind and staggered through darkness. Nightmare figures loomed before me: Paris Paradise, his body a broken, bloody mess from his encounter with the wheeler, babbling, "I told you so, I told you so," through the red, toothless ruin of his mouth; Paul Jarez, glistening with sweat as his body spun in an endless series of pirouettes beneath a head that never moved. I dodged them both and ran on.

Marcel dropped from the darkness above me, chest soaked in scarlet from the knife wounds that killed him, eyes blank and dead. I pushed him aside, sobbing with horror and pain, but he grabbed my ankle and almost pulled me down. I screamed and kicked. My boot hit his face with a sickening crunch. He let go, and I ran on.

But my pain waxed, growing far, far worse, and then, suddenly, I saw movement ahead—tentacles, thousands of disembodied, red-orange tentacles, filling the corridor, dropping from the ceiling, slithering toward me. I turned to run the other way and saw more tentacles behind me, an army of them, some ending in purple, slit-pupilled Hydran eyes, glittering and cold.

They moved slowly, but there were so many—I couldn't escape them all!

Or maybe I could have, if not for the pain. But when I tried to dash to freedom, agony hit me like a riot club thudding into my gut. I doubled over, gasping, and the tentacles had me, coiling around my arms and legs and neck and body, dragging me down, though I thrashed and screamed till my throat bled.

From nowhere, another of the monsters from the cages appeared. It opened its horrible mouth, and once more I felt fangs sink into my arm. Numbness seized me. I couldn't move. The creature vanished, and the tentacles uncoiled and assembled themselves into a complete hydra—Rain, standing over me with a hypodermic.

Meta appeared beside him, looking down. Betrayed! She'd joined forces with Rain, she'd sold me out...I wanted to howl curses at her, but I couldn't open my mouth.

"What else can we do?" Meta boomed in an incongruous bass.

"I can think of only one thing," said Rain, his voice even deeper and slower. "The time pocket."

No! Paul Jerez, frozen forever—Paris Paradise, crazed and ancient at nineteen—how could I have thought Meta was my friend? Streetsense had been right. Don't make friends. Don't trust people. Look after yourself. I'd trusted her, and she...she...

The numbness gripped me tighter, and vision faded. I wandered through a barren land of flat grey rock and flat grey skies and cold, skin-drenching rain, a land where nothing changed...until, hours or days or even years later, it began to grow dark.

Nightfall, I thought. *I can sleep. I can escape the pain.* Though distant and muffled, it was still there, tormenting me. *I can rest…*

But some spark within me, the spark that had driven me out of the orphanage to begin with, maybe, blazed up against the darkness. A ragged scarecrow figure appeared, carrying a battered stringsynth. The face, blurred at first, came into focus.

I stared at myself, at Kit, as I had been before Sensation Singles' computers gave birth to Andy Nebula. "Death, not rest, Nebula," he snarled at me. "Death lies down this road."

"Rest," I insisted.

I tried to push past, but he pushed back, hard, then unslung the stringsynth, holding it like a club. "Death!" Kit swung the stringsynth at me, forcing me to stagger back. "That's the easy way out, Nebula, and I won't let you take it. You do, and The Dealer wins. Qualls wins. Rain wins. And I don't owe them any favours."

"The Dealer's dead."

"So why are you in such a hurry to join him?" He jabbed me in the chest with the stringsynth, sending me sprawling back onto my butt. I scramble up, feeling anger, feeling, in fact, the first emotion I had felt since coming to this grey land. The sky grew a little bit lighter.

Kit jabbed me with the stringsynth again, and again I fell backward. This time he put his foot on my chest and shoved me hard to the ground. "Coward," he said contemptuously. "No guts." He leaned over and glared down at me. "Go on, then. Die. It's what you deserve, streetslime." He spat in my face. "You're nothing. You've always been a nothing!"

"I'm a musician! That's not a nothing."

"You? Caterwauling, shrieking—you call that music? People paid you just so you'd shut up, you useless piece of—"

My smouldering anger exploded into blood-boiling rage. I lunged upward. My fingers closed on his throat. I could feel his pulse pounding under my thumbs—and then he melted away, along with the mist and the darkness and the flat grey plain, and I found myself upright in a bed, reaching out with my hands, wires trailing from my head and chest, alarms going off all around me, and half a dozen people staring at me.

Somebody was screaming. I closed my mouth, and the sound stopped. The room spun around me, I felt weak as a naked baby rat, and I hurt—all over, I hurt—but I lived. I lived!

I lay back and took deep breaths of air, and people suddenly surrounded me. Real people. Two men, two women. Not hydras. All in white. And this antiseptic white room—a hospital. "Where—" I began, and had to swallow and begin again. "Where am I?"

A very tall woman with white hair leaned down. "Carstair's Folly."

"Carstair's..." But that was impossible—unless—maybe the old flashman had attacked me, hit me on the head, and everything else had been a dream—

Meta pushed her way between two doctors, an enormous grin splitting her face. "You're alive! You're all right!"

Carstair's Folly—and Meta. She hadn't betrayed me. She'd saved me again. She really was a friend! I felt ashamed of my doubts—and fiercely, fiercely happy that I'd been wrong. "I've been better," I croaked. "But, yeah...I think I am all right."

"No, you're not," said the tall woman severely. "You've been in a coma for two weeks, you're dehydrated, you're still suffering from withdrawal symptoms, and I don't like the looks of your heartbeat. You've got a lot of recovering to do yet, young man." Meta gave her such a concerned look that her face softened. "But you're *going* to be all right. And you can think your friends for being smart enough to put you in stasis until they could get you to a human hospital. Otherwise..." She raised her voice. "Everyone out! He needs rest and a little food that doesn't come through a tube in his arm. Nurse Coles, will you..."

Friends? Plural? "What does she mean, friends?" I asked Meta over the excited babble of the medicos' voices.

One voice carried back to me. "Strangest thing I ever saw! His vital signs were dropping off, I'd have sworn he was dying, then all of a sudden he lunges up and..." The door cut him off.

"I couldn't have gotten you here by myself," Meta said. "It was Rain who thought of putting you in stasis."

"Rain?" I remembered that. But I'd thought...but if I was here... "I don't understand. Rain was in league with The Dealer. He tried to trap me at Fat Sloan's—he—I saw him take flash, and watch Paul Jerez dance. I thought..." My voice trailed off. I thought she'd betrayed me to him, but I couldn't tell her that.

Meta laughed. "We had it all wrong, Kit. He wasn't trying to trap you. He wanted to warn you. He knew what was going on."

"But I—"

"Look, he'll have to explain it himself. He'll be here any minute. And you shouldn't get so worked up. I'm sure it's not good for you." Her voice softened. "Don't you dare do anything to mess yourself up like that again."

"All right." But in fact, far from feeling worse, I felt more buoyant than ever. Meta hadn't sold me out—and neither had

Rain. I didn't just have one friend, I had two! Orbital! "Well, can you at least tell me what happened after you and Rain sedated me?"

"You recognized us?" She looked surprised. "You kept babbling on about tentacles and—"

"I recognized you. For a moment. But what happened next?"

With frequent interruptions on my part, she told me. Afraid I might die, they'd put me in stasis with Paul, then, once we reached Hydra, loaded both of us onto a high-speed human luxury liner heading to the Pleasure Planets. Paul, addicted to flash but otherwise unharmed, had had to go through withdrawal. "He's all right now," Meta said, "except he says he'll never dance again."

I shuddered, thinking of what he'd been forced to do. "I don't blame him."

I'd been kept in their medical bay during the five-day trip, but their doctors and medical computers had had no more idea of how to treat me than the hydras had. No human had ever been bitten by the flashdevil (Meta's word, which seemed likely to stick) before. Meta had contacted her parents, who had understandably been very glad to hear from her, and told them in no uncertain terms to have the best doctors waiting when I arrived. Her father hadn't been eager to roll out the red carpet— or even the white hospital bed—for me, I gathered, and I guess I couldn't blame him, but Meta had insisted—which apparently shocked him. "First time I ever stood up to him," she said thoughtfully. "I've always been scared of him. But this time, I didn't care. And you know, he really was worried about me. I was kind of surprised."

"You're lucky to have someone to worry about you," I said. "I never did."

"You do now," Meta said.

The doctors on Carstair's Folly had found me a fascinating case, apparently. Lots of brain activity, but never waking up—as though I were in a permanent dream state. But today... "They told me you were dying," Meta said soberly. "They said they didn't expect you to last more than a few hours. I came right away." She touched my hand. "I cried," she said softly.

I had a lump in my own throat. "I'm sorry."

"Well, it's not your fault. It was The Dealer's."

"What happened to him? And the other hydra? Are they dead?"

"No, gladeye! Dead, they are not!" chortled a new voice.

"Rain?" I raised up a little and saw my Hydran friend in the doorway.

"Orbital that you are awake, gladeye." Rain placed a tentacle on my bare shoulder. "I have sworn to retain memory of you. I am glad I may still be able to add some new ones."

"I'm glad you'll be able to, too," I said fervently, "but right now I'm more interested in answers than memories. How did you know about Qualls and the Dealer? What were you doing on The Dealer's ship? Who are you?"

"I am an enforcement agent for the legislative council of Hydra," Rain said.

"What?"

"He's a 'forcer," Meta translated helpfully.

"A 'forcer?"

"A 'forcer, gladeye! Flash is illegal on our planet, as on yours, and the Dealer was the source of much of it. I had been trailing him for some time when I met you. I knew about his deals with Qualls, and my sources close to Qualls told me he had you in mind as the next Sensation Single. So I, as you would say, 'flopped' at Fat Sloan's." Rain made a strange hissing sound. "He was most willing to take my money to ensure you would share my room the next time you came by. I do not think he is a very law-abiding hostelry host."

I laughed. "No. No, he definitely isn't."

"I waited four nights, and then it rained, and there you were. I made sure Qualls found you at the Spaceport. I paid close attention to your musical career."

He warbled—badly—a couple of lines from "From the Street to the Stars." Manfully, I did not wince.

"When you came back to Fistfight City," he continued, "I knew a deal between The Dealer and Qualls had been made. I tried to contact you before they sealed it, hoping you could get me onto *The Bullet* so I could be there when that happened. But you did not join me at Fat Sloan's, and when The Dealer booked passage on a commercial ship, I knew I must act expeditiously. I decided you must have realized something was wrong and escaped Qualls. I had to remain with The Dealer. I booked onto the same ship as him, and set about convincing him I would be a valuable customer."

"But I saw you take the flash!"

"An illusion. What you would call sleight-of-hand." He held up a tentacle and wriggled its tip.

I laughed, though it hurt. "You said The Dealer and that other hydra aren't dead? Then what happened to them?"

Rain's tentacles squirmed. "You know how flash affects us?"

"It makes you forget what you have just experienced. Yes, Qualls explained it."

"Not to *me!*" Meta complained.

I hushed her. "I'll tell you later."

"That is a single small dose," said Rain. "The bite of the—what did you call it, Meta?"

"The flashdevil!"

"—the flashdevil—is far, far worse, as you have reason to know. The Dealer, his employee—they lost all memories. Forever. They are no longer the people they were. They are no longer people at all."

"Can't say I'm sorry," I muttered. I closed my eyes, feeling very tired. "I'm glad that's over."

"Don't you want to hear about Qualls?" said Meta.

"Meta, we should—" Rain began, but I opened my eyes. "What about him?"

"Arrested for fraud, murder, kidnapping, and half a dozen other crimes," Meta said. "And your credit has been unfrozen. *And* you've attracted so much media attention that there are half a dozen promoters here on Carstair's Folly just waiting to sponsor your first non-Single concert once you're recovered. You're going to be a star again, Andy Nebula!"

I sighed and closed my eyes again, this time in final, complete satisfaction. "Never heard of him. My name's Kit."

THE END

EDWARD WILLETT is the author of more than sixty books of science fiction, fantasy, and nonfiction for readers of all ages. *Marseguro* (DAW Books) won the Aurora Award (honouring Canadian science fiction and fantasy) for Best Long-Form Work in English in 2009. His young adult fantasy *Spirit Singer* (recently rereleased by Shadowpaw Press) won the Regina Book Award for best book by a Regina author at the 2002 Saskatchewan Book Awards. Several other of his books have been shortlisted for those and other awards.

Ed's most recent novels are *Worldshaper, Master of the World,* and *The Moonlit World,* the first three books in the *Worldshapers* series (DAW Books). Other recent titles include *The Cityborn* and the *Masks of Aygrima* trilogy (written as E.C. Blake), also from DAW; for Bundoran Press, the *Peregrine Rising* duology (*Right to Know* and *Falcon's Egg*)' and for Coteau Books, the five-book *Shards of Excalibur* young-adult fantasy series. His nonfiction runs the gamut from science books to biographies to history. He hosts *The Worldshapers* podcast (theworldshapers.com), winner of the Aurora Award for Best Fan Related Work, in which he talks to other science fiction and fantasy authors about their creative process.

Born in Silver City, New Mexico, Ed moved to Saskatchewan from Texas at the age of eight, and grew up in Weyburn, where his father taught at Western Christian College. He earned a BA in journalism from Harding University in Searcy, Arkansas, and returned to Weyburn to begin his career at the weekly *Weyburn Review*, first as a reporter/photographer/columnist/cartoonist, and eventually as news editor. He moved to Regina in 1988 as communications officer for the then-fledgling Saskatchewan Science Centre. He began writing full-time in 1993.

For most of two decades, Ed wrote a weekly science column that appeared in the *Regina LeaderPost* and other newspapers, and talked about science weekly on CBC Saskatchewan's *Afternoon Edition* radio program.

In addition to being a writer, Ed is a professional actor and singer who has performed in numerous plays, musicals, and operas, and sung in several auditioned choirs, including the Canadian Chamber Choir. He lives in Regina, Saskatchewan, with his wife, Margaret Anne Hodges, P. Eng., a past president of the Association of Professional Engineers and Geoscientists of Saskatchewan. They have one daughter, Alice, and a black Siberian cat, Shadowpaw.

You can find Ed online at www.edwardwillett.com.

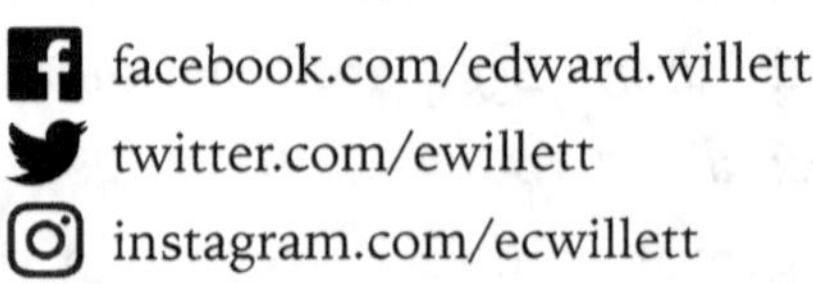

From Bundoran Press

PEREGRINE RISING

Right to Know

Falcon's Egg

————

From Coteau Books

THE SHARDS OF EXCALIBUR

Song of the Sword

Twist of the Blade

Lake in the Clouds

Cave Beneath the Sea

Door into Faerie

————

From Shadowpaw Press

Paths to the Stars

Spirit Singer

————

From Your Nickel's Worth Publishing

I Tumble through the Diamond Dust:

A Collection of Fantastical Poems